THE RANGE DWELLERS

B. M. BOWER

1st WORLD
LIBRARY
Literary Society

The Range Dwellers

B. M. Bower

© 1st World Library – Literary Society, 2004
PO Box 2211
Fairfield, IA 52556
www.1stworldlibrary.org
First Edition

LCCN: 2005901132

Softcover ISBN: 1-4218-1110-3
Hardcover ISBN: 1-4218-1010-7
eBook ISBN: 1-4218-1210-X

Purchase *"The Range Dwellers"*
as a traditional bound book at:
www.1stWorldLibrary.org/purchase.asp?ISBN=1-4218-1110-3

1st World Library Literary Society is a nonprofit organization dedicated to promoting literacy by:

- Creating a free internet library accessible from any computer worldwide.
- Hosting writing competitions and offering book publishing scholarships.

Readers interested in supporting literacy through sponsorship, donations or membership please contact: literacy@1stworldlibrary.org Check us out at: www.1stworldlibrary.ORG and start downloading free ebooks today.

The Range Dwellers
contributed by Tim, Ed & Rodney
in support of
1st World Library Literary Society

CONTENTS

CHAPTER I.

THE REWARD OF FOLLY.

I'm something like the old maid you read about - the one who always knows all about babies and just how to bring them up to righteous maturity; I've got a mighty strong conviction that I know heaps that my dad never thought of about the proper training for a healthy male human. I don't suppose I'll ever have a chance to demonstrate my wisdom, but, if I do, there are a few things that won't happen to my boy.

If I've got a comfortable wad of my own, the boy shall have his fun without any nagging, so long as he keeps clean and honest. He shall go to any college he may choose - and right here is where my wisdom will sit up and get busy. If I'm fool enough to let that kid have more money than is healthy for him, and if I go to sleep while he's wising up to the art of making it fade away without leaving anything behind to tell the tale, and learning a lot of habits that aren't doing him any good, I won't come down on him with both feet and tell him all the different brands of fool he's been, and mourn because the Lord in His mercy laid upon me this burden of an unregenerate son. I shall try and remember that he's the son of his father, and not expect too much of him. It's long odds I shall find points of resemblance a-plenty between us - and the more cussedness he develops, the more I shall see myself in him reflected.

I don't mean to be hard on dad. He was always good to me, in his way. He's got more things than a son to look after, and as that son is supposed to have a normal allowance of gray matter and is no physical weakling, he probably took it for granted that the son could look after himself - which the mines and railroads and ranches that represent his millions can't.

But it wasn't giving me a square deal. He gave me an allowance and paid my debts besides, and let me amble through school at my own gait - which wasn't exactly slow - and afterward let me go. If I do say it, I had lived a fairly decent sort of life. I belonged to some good clubs - athletic, mostly - and trained regularly, and was called a fair boxer among the amateurs. I could tell to a glass - after a lot of practise - just how much of 'steen different brands I could take without getting foolish, and I could play poker and win once in awhile. I had a steam-yacht and a motor of my own, and it was generally stripped to racing trim. And I wasn't tangled up with any women; actress-worship had never appealed to me. My tastes all went to the sporting side of life and left women to the fellows with less nerve and more sentiment.

So I had lived for twenty-five years - just having the best time a fellow with an unlimited resource can have, if he is healthy.

It was then, on my twenty-fifth birthday, that I walked into dad's private library with a sonly smile, ready for the good wishes and the check that I was in the habit of getting - I'd been unlucky, and Lord knows I needed it! - and what does the dear man do?

Instead of one check, he handed me a sheaf of them, each stamped in divers places by divers banks. I flipped the ends and looked them over a bit, because I saw that was what he expected of me; but the truth is, checks don't interest me much after they've been messed up with red and green stamps. They're about as enticing as a last year's popular song.

Dad crossed his legs, matched his finger-tips together, and looked at me over his glasses. Many a man knows that attitude and that look, and so many a man has been as uncomfortable as I began to be, and has felt as keen a sense of impending trouble. I began immediately searching my memory for some especial brand of devilment that I'd been sampling, but there was nothing doing. I had been losing some at poker lately, and I'd been away to the bad out at Ingleside; still, I looked him innocently in the eye and wondered what was coming.

"That last check is worthy of particular attention," he said dryly. "The others are remarkable only for their size and continuity of numbers; but that last one should be framed and hung upon the wall at the foot of your bed, though you would not see it often. I consider it a diploma of your qualification as Master Jackanapes." (Dad's vocabulary, when he is angry, contains some rather strengthy words of the old-fashioned type.)

I looked at the check and began to see light. I *had* been a bit rollicky that time. It wasn't drawn for very much, that check; I've lost more on one jack-pot, many a time, and thought nothing of it. And, though the events leading up to it were a bit rapid and undignified, perhaps, I couldn't see anything to get excited over, as I could see dad plainly was.

"For a young man twenty-five years old and with brains enough - supposedly - to keep out of the feeble-minded class, it strikes me you indulge in some damned poor pastimes," went on dad disagreeably. "Cracking champagne-bottles in front of the Cliff House - on a Sunday at that - may be diverting to the bystanders, but it can hardly be called dignified, and I fail to see how it is going to fit a man for any useful business."

Business? Lord! dad never had mentioned a useful business to me before. I felt my eyelids fly up; this was springing birthday surprises with a vengeance.

"Driving an automobile on forbidden roads, being arrested and fined - on Sunday, at that -"

"Now, look here, dad," I cut in, getting a bit hot under the collar myself, "by all the laws of nature, there must have been a time when *you* were twenty-five years old and cut a little swath of your own. And, seeing you're as big as your offspring - six-foot-one, and you can't deny it - and fairly husky for a man of your age, I'll bet all you dare that said swath was not of the narrow-gage variety. I've never heard of your teaching a class in any Sunday-school, and if you never drove your machine beyond the dead-line and cracked champagne-bottles on the wheels in front of the Cliff House, it's because automobiles weren't invented and Cliff House wasn't built. Begging your pardon, dad - I'll bet you were a pretty rollicky young blade, yourself."

Now dad is very old-fashioned in some of his notions; one of them is that a parent may hand out a roast that will frizzle the foliage for blocks around, and, guilty or innocent, the son must take it, as he'd take cod-liver oil - it's-nasty-but-good-for-what-ails-you. He snapped his mouth shut, and, being his son and having that habit myself, I recognized the symptoms and judged that things would presently grow interesting.

I was betting on a full-house. The atmosphere grew tense. I heard a lot of things in the next five minutes that no one but my dad could say without me trying mighty hard to make him swallow them. And I just sat there and looked at him and took it.

I couldn't agree with him that I'd committed a grievous crime. It wasn't much of a lark, as larks go: just an incident at the close of a rather full afternoon. Coming around up the beach front Ingleside House a few days before, in the *Yellow Peril* - my machine - we got to badgering each other about doing things not orthodox. At last Barney MacTague dared me to drive the *Yellow Peril* past the dead-line - down by the Pavilion - and on up the hill to Sutro Baths. Naturally, I couldn't take a dare like that, and went him one better; I told him I'd not only drive to the very top of the hill, but I'd stop at the Gift House and crack a bottle of champagne on each wheel of the *Yellow*

Peril, in honor of the occasion; that would make a bottle apiece, for there were four of us along.

It was done, to the delight of the usual Sunday crowd of brides, grooms, tourists, and kids. A mounted policeman interviewed us, to the further delight of the crowd, and invited us to call upon a certain judge whom none of us knew. We did so, and dad was good enough to pay the fine, which, as I said before, was not much. I've had less fun for more money, often.

Dad didn't say anything at the time, so I was not looking for the roast I was getting. It appeared, from his view-point, that I was about as useless, imbecile, and utterly no-account a son as a man ever had, and if there was anything good in me it was not visible except under a strong magnifying-glass.

He said, among other things too painful to mention, that he was getting old - dad is about fifty-six - and that if I didn't buck up and amount to something soon, he didn't know what was to become of the business.

Then he delivered the knockout blow that he'd been working up to. He was going to see what there was in me, he said. He would pay my bills, and, as a birthday gift, he would present me with a through ticket to Osage, in Montana - where he owned a ranch called the Bay State - and a stock-saddle, spurs, chaps, and a hundred dollars. After that I must work out my own salvation - or the other thing. If I wanted more money inside a year or two, I would have to work for it just as if I were an orphan without a dad who writes checks on demand. He said that there was always something to do on the Bay State Ranch - which is one of dad's places. I could do as I pleased, he said, but he'd advise me to buckle down and learn something about cattle. It was plain I never would amount to anything in an office. He laid a yard or two of ticket on the table at my elbow, and on top of that a check for one hundred dollars, payable to one Ellis Carleton.

I took up the check and read every word on it twice - not

because I needed to; I was playing for time to think. Then I twisted it up in a taper, held it to the blaze in the fireplace, and lighted a cigarette with it. Dad kept his finger-tips together and watched me without any expression whatsoever in his face. I took three deliberate puffs, picked up the ticket, and glanced along down its dirty green length. Dad never moved a muscle, and I remember the clock got to ticking louder than I'd ever heard it in my life before. I may as well be perfectly honest! That ticket did not appeal to me a little bit. I think he expected to see that go up in smoke, also. But, though I'm pretty much of a fool at times, I believe there are lucid intervals when I recognize certain objects - such as justice. I knew that, in the main, dad was right. I *had* been leading a rather reckless existence, and I was getting pretty old for such kid foolishness. He had measured out the dose, and I meant to swallow it without whining - but it was exceeding bitter to the palate!

"I see the ticket is dated twenty-four hours ahead," I said as calmly as I knew how, "which gives me time to have Rankin pack a few duds. I hope the outfit you furnish includes a red silk handkerchief and a Colt's .44 revolver, and a key to the proper method of slaying acquaintances in the West. I hate to start in with all white chips."

"You probably mean a Colt's .45," said dad, with a more convincing calmness than I could show. "It shall be provided. As to the key, you will no doubt find that on the ground when you arrive."

"Very well," I replied, getting up and stretching my arms up as high as I could reach - which was beastly manners, of course, but a safe vent for my feelings, which cried out for something or somebody to punch. "You've called the turn, and I'll go. It may be many moons ere we two meet again - and when we do, the crime of cracking my own champagne - for I paid for it, you know - on my own automobile wheels may not seem the heinous thing it looks now. See you later, dad."

I walked out with my head high in the air and my spirits rather low, if the truth must be told. Dad was generally kind and wise and generous, but he certainly did break out in unexpected places sometimes. Going to the Bay State Ranch, just at that time, was not a cheerful prospect. San Francisco and Seattle were just starting a series of ballgames that promised to be rather swift, and I'd got a lot up on the result. I hated to go just then. And Montana has the reputation of being rather beastly in early March - I knew that much.

I caught a car down to the Olympic, hunted up Barney MacTague, and played poker with him till two o'clock that night, and never once mentioned the trip I was contemplating. Then I went home, routed up my man, and told him what to pack, and went to bed for a few hours; if there was anything pleasant in my surroundings that I failed to think of as I lay there, it must be very trivial indeed. I even went so far as to regret leaving Ethel Mapleton, whom I cared nothing for.

And above all and beneath all, hanging in the background of my mind and dodging forward insistently in spite of myself, was a deep resentment - a soreness against dad for the way he had served me. Granted I was wild and a useless cumberer of civilization; I was only what my environments had made me. Dad had let me run, and he had never kicked on the price of my folly, or tried to pull me up at the start. He had given his time to his mines and his cattle-ranches and railroads, and had left his only son to go to the devil if he chose and at his own pace. Then, because the son had come near making a thorough job of it, he had done - *this*. I felt hardly used and at odds with life, during those last few hours in the little old burgh.

All the next day I went the pace as usual with the gang, and at seven, after an early dinner, caught a down-town car and set off alone to the ferry. I had not seen dad since I left him in the library, and I did not particularly wish to see him, either. Possibly I had some unfilial notion of making him ashamed and sorry. It is even possible that I half-expected him to come and apologize, and offer to let things go on in the old way. In that event I was prepared to be chesty. I would look at him coldly and say: "You have seen fit to buy me a ticket to Osage, Montana. So be it; to Osage, Montana, am I bound." Oh, I had it all fixed!

Dad came into the ferry waiting-room just as the passengers were pouring off the boat, and sat down beside me as if nothing had happened. He did not look sad, or contrite, or ashamed - not, at least, enough to notice. He glanced at his watch, and then handed me a letter.

"There," he began briskly, "that is to Perry Potter, the Bay State foreman. I have wired him that you are on the way."

The gate went up at that moment, and he stood up and held out his hand. "Sorry I can't go over with you," he said. "I've an important meeting to attend. Take care of yourself, Ellie boy."

I gripped his hand warmly, though I had intended to give him a dead-fish sort of shake. After all, he was my dad, and there were just us two. I picked up my suit-case and started for the gate. I looked back once, and saw dad standing there gazing after me - and he did not look particularly brisk. Perhaps, after all, dad cared more than he let on. It's a way the Carletons have, I have heard.

CHAPTER II.

THE WHITE DIVIDE.

If a phrenologist should undertake to "read" my head, he would undoubtedly find my love of home - if that is what it is called - a sharply defined welt. I know that I watched the lights of old Frisco slip behind me with as virulent a case of the deeps as often comes to a man when his digestion is good. It wasn't that I could not bear the thought of hardship; I've taken hunting trips up into the mountains more times than I can remember, and ate ungodly messes of my own invention, and waded waist-deep in snow and slept under the stars, and enjoyed nearly every minute. So it wasn't the hardships that I had every reason to expect that got me down. I think it was the feeling that dad had turned me down; that I was in exile, and - in his eyes, at least - disgraced, it was knowing that he thought me pretty poor truck, without giving me a chance to be anything better. I humped over the rail at the stern, and watched the waves slap at us viciously, like an ill-tempered poodle, and felt for all the world like a dog that's been kicked out into the rain. Maybe the medicine was good for me, but it wasn't pleasant. It never occurred to me, that night, to wonder how dad felt about it; but I've often thought of it since.

I had a section to myself, so I could sulk undisturbed; dad was not small, at any rate, and, though he hadn't let me have his car, he meant me to be decently comfortable. That first night I slept without a break; the second I sat in the smoker till a most unrighteous hour, cultivating the acquaintance of a drummer for a rubber-goods outfit. I thought that, seeing I was about to mingle with the working classes, I couldn't begin too soon to study them. He was a pretty good sort, too.

The rubber-goods man left me at Seattle, and from there on I was at the tender mercies of my own thoughts and an elderly lady with a startlingly blond daughter, who sat directly opposite me and was frankly disposed to friendliness. I had never given much time to the study of women, and so had no alternative but to answer questions and smile fatuously upon the blond daughter, and wonder if I ought to warn the mother that "clothes do not make the man," and that I was a black sheep and not a desirable acquaintance. Before I had quite settled that point, they left the train. I am afraid I am not distinctly a chivalrous person; I hummed the Doxology after their retreating forms and retired into myself, with a feeling that my own society is at times desirable and greatly to be chosen.

After that I was shy, and nothing happened except that on the last evening of the trip, I gave up my sole remaining five dollars in the diner, and walked out whistling softly. I was utterly and unequivocally strapped. I went into the smoker to think it over; I knew I had started out with a hundred or so, and that I had considered that sufficient to see me through. Plainly, it was not sufficient; but it is a fact that I looked upon it as a joke, and went to sleep grinning idiotically at the thought of me, Ellis Carleton, heir to almost as many millions as I was years old, without the price of a breakfast in his pocket. It seemed novel and interesting, and I rather enjoyed the situation. I wasn't hungry, then!

Osage, Montana, failed to rouse any enthusiasm in me when I saw the place next day, except that it offered possibilities in the way of eating - at least, I fancied it did, until I stepped down upon the narrow platform and looked about me. It was two o'clock in the afternoon, and I had fasted since dinner the evening before. I was not happy.

B. M. BOWER

I began to see where I might have economized a bit, and so have gone on eating regularly to the end of the journey. I reflected that stewed terrapin, for instance, might possibly be considered an extravagance under the circumstances; and a fellow sentenced to honest toil and exiled to the wilderness should not, it seemed to me then, cause his table to be sprinkled, quite so liberally as I had done, with tall glasses - nor need he tip the porter quite so often or so generously. A dollar looked bigger to me, just then, than a wheel of the *Yellow Peril*. I began to feel unkindly toward that porter! he had looked so abominably well-fed and sleek, and he had tips that I would be glad to feel in my own pocket again. I stood alone upon the platform and gazed wistfully after the retreating train; many people have done that before me, if one may believe those who write novels, and for once in my life I felt a bond of sympathy between us. It's safe betting that I did more solid thinking on frenzied finance in the five minutes I stood there watching that train slid off beyond the sky-line than I'd done in all my life before. I'd heard, of course, about fellows getting right down to cases, but I'd never personally experienced the sensation. I'd always had money - or, if I hadn't, I knew where to go. And dad had caught me when I'd all but overdrawn my account at the bank. I was always doing that, for dad paid the bills. That last night with Barney MacTague hadn't been my night to win, and I'd dropped quite a lot there. And - oh, what's the use? I was broke, all right enough, and I was hungry enough to eat the proverbial crust.

It seemed to me it might be a good idea to hunt up the gentleman named Perry Potter, whom dad called his foreman. I turned around and caught a tall, brown-faced native studying my back with grave interest. He didn't blush when I looked him in the eye, but smiled a tired smile and said he reckoned I was the chap he'd been sent to meet. There was no welcome in his voice, I noticed. I looked him over critically.

"Are you the gentleman with the alliterative cognomen?" I asked him airily, hoping he would be puzzled.

He was not, evidently. "Perry Potter? He's at the ranch." He was damnably tolerant, and I said nothing. I hate to make the same sort of fool of myself twice. So when he proposed that we "hit the trail," I followed meekly in his wake. He did not offer to take my suit-case, and I was about to remind him of the oversight when it occurred to me that possibly he was not a servant - he certainly didn't act like one. I carried my own suitcase - which was, I have thought since, the only wise move I had made since I left home.

A strong but unsightly spring-wagon, with mud six inches deep on the wheels, seemed the goal, and we trailed out to it, picking up layers of soil as we went. The ground did not *look* muddy, but it was; I have since learned that that particular phase of nature's hypocrisy is called "doby." I don't admire it, myself. I stopped by the wagon and scraped my shoes on the cleanest spoke I could find, and swore. My guide untied the horses, gathered up the reins, and sought a spoke on his side of the wagon; he looked across at me with a gleam of humanity in his eyes - the first I had seen there.

"It sure beats hell the way it hangs on," he remarked, and from that minute I liked him. It was the first crumb of sympathy that had fallen to me for days, and you can bet I appreciated it.

We got in, and he pulled a blanket over our knees and picked up the whip. It wasn't a stylish turnout - I had seen farmers driving along the railroad-track in rigs like it, and I was surprised at dad for keeping such a layout. Fact is, I didn't think much of dad, anyway, about that time.

"How far is it to the Bay State Ranch?" I asked.

"One hundred and forty miles, air-line," said he casually. "The train was late, so I reckon we better stop over till morning. There's a town over the hill, and a hotel that beats nothing a long way."

A hundred and forty miles from the station, "air-line,"

B. M. BOWER

sounded to me like a pretty stiff proposition to go up against; also, how was a fellow going to put up at a hotel when he hadn't the coin? Would my mysterious guide be shocked to learn that John A. Carleton's son and heir had landed in a strange land without two-bits to his name? Jerusalem! I couldn't have paid street-car fare down-town; I couldn't even have bought a paper on the street. While I was remembering all the things a millionaire's son can't do if he happens to be without a nickel in his pocket, we pulled up before a place that, for the sake of propriety, I am willing to call a hotel; at the time, I remember, I had another name for it.

"In case I might get lost in this strange city," I said to my companion as I jumped out, "I'd like to know what people call you when they're in a good humor."

He grinned down at me. "Frosty Miller would hit me, all right," he informed me, and drove off somewhere down the street. So I went in and asked for a room, and got it.

This sounds sordid, I know, but the truth must be told, though the artistic sense be shocked. Barred from the track as I was, sent out to grass in disgrace while the little old world kept moving without me to help push, my mind passed up all the things I might naturally be supposed to dwell upon and stuck to three little no-account grievances that I hate to tell about now. They look small, for a fact, now that they're away out of sight, almost, in the past; but they were quite big enough at the time to give me a bad hour or two. The biggest one was the state of my appetite; next, and not more than a nose behind, was the state of my pockets; and the last was, had Rankin packed the gray tweed trousers that I had a liking for, or had he not? I tried to remember whether I had spoken to him about them, and I sat down on the edge of the bed in that little box of a room, took my head between my fists, and called Rankin several names he sometimes deserved and had frequently heard from my lips. I'd have given a good deal to have Rankin at my elbow just then.

They were not in the suit-case - or, if they were, I had not run across them. Rankin had a way of stowing things away so that even he had to do some tall searching, and he had another way of filling up my suit-cases with truck I'd no immediate use for. I yanked the case toward me, unlocked it, and turned it out on the bed, just to prove Rankin's general incapacity as valet to a fastidious fellow like me.

There was the suit I had worn on that memorable excursion to the Cliff House - I had told Rankin to pitch it into the street, for I had discovered Teddy Van Greve in one almost exactly like it, and - Hello! Rankin had certainly overlooked a bet. I never caught him at it before, that's certain. He had a way of coming to my left elbow, and, in a particularly virtuous tone, calling my attention to the fact that I had left several loose bills in my pockets. Rankin was that honest I often told him he would land behind the bars as an embezzler some day. But Rankin had done it this time, for fair; tucked away in a pocket of the waistcoat was money - real, legal, lawful tender - m-o-n-e-y! I don't suppose the time will ever come when it will look as good to me as it did right then. I held those bank-notes - there were two of them, double XX's - to my face and sniffed them like I'd never seen the like before and never expected to again. And the funny part was that I forgot all about wanting the gray trousers, and all about the faults of Rankin. My feet were on bottom again, and my head on top. I marched down-stairs, whistling, with my hands in my pockets and my chin in the air, and told the landlord to serve dinner an hour earlier than usual, and to make it a good one.

He looked at me with a curious mixture of wonder and amusement. "Dinner," he drawled calmly, "has been over for three hours; but I guess we can give yuh some supper any time after five."

I suppose he looked upon me as the rankest kind of a tenderfoot. I calculated the time of my torture till I might, without embarrassing explanations, partake of a much-needed repast, and went to the door; waiting was never my long suit, and I had thoughts of getting outside and taking a look around. At the second step I changed my mind - there was that deceptive mud to reckon with.

So from the doorway I surveyed all of Montana that lay between me and the sky-line, and decided that my bets would remain on California. The sky was a dull slate, tumbled into what looked like rain-clouds and depressing to the eye. The land was a dull yellowish-brown, with a purple line of hills off to the south, and with untidy snow-drifts crouching in the hollows. That was all, so far as I could see, and if dulness and an unpeopled wilderness make for the reformation of man, it struck me that I was in a fair way to become a saint if I stayed here long. I had heard the cattle-range called picturesque; I couldn't see the joke.

Frosty Miller sat opposite me at table when, in the course of human events, I ate again, and the way I made the biscuit and ham and boiled potatoes vanish filled him with astonishment, if one may judge a man's feelings by the size of his eyes. I told him that the ozone of the plains had given me an appetite, and he did not contradict me; he looked at my plate, and then smiled at his own, and said nothing - which was polite of him.

"Did you ever skip two meals and try to make it up on the third?" I asked him when we went out, and he said "Sure," and rolled a cigarette. In those first hours of our acquaintance Frosty was not what I'd call loquacious.

That night I took out the letter addressed to one Perry Potter, which dad had given me and which I had not had time to seal in his presence, and read it cold-bloodedly. I don't do such things as a rule, but I was getting a suspicion that I was being queered; that I'd got to start my exile under a handicap of the contempt of the natives. If dad had stacked the deck on me, I wanted to know it. But I misjudged him - or, perhaps, he knew I'd read it. All he had written wouldn't hurt the reputation of any one. It was:

The bearer, Ellis H. Carleton, is my son. He will probably be with you for some time, and will not try to assume any authority or usurp your position as foreman and overseer. You will treat him as you do the other boys, and if he wants to work, pay him the same wages - if he earns them.

It wasn't exactly throwing flowers in the path my young feet should tread, but it might have been worse. At least, he did not give Perry Potter his unbiased opinion of me, and it left me with a free hand to warp their judgment somewhat in my favor. But - "If he wants to work, pay him the same wages - if he earns them." Whew!

I might have saved him the trouble of writing that, if I had only known it. Dad could go too far in this thing, I told myself chestily. I had come, seeing that he insisted upon it, but I'd be damned if I'd work for any man with a circus-poster name, and have him lord it over me. I hadn't been brought up to appreciate that kind of joke. I meant to earn my living, but I did not mean to get out and slave for Perry Potter. There must be something respectable for a man to do in this country besides ranch work.

In the morning we started off, with my trunks in the wagon, toward the line of purple hills in the south. Frosty Miller told me, when I asked him, that they were forty-eight miles away, that they marked the Missouri River, and that we would stop there overnight. That, if I remember, was about the extent of our conversation that day. We smoked cigarettes - Frosty Miller made his, one by one, as he needed them - and thought our own thoughts. I rather suspect our thoughts were a good many miles apart, though our shoulders touched. When you think of it, people may rub elbows and still have an ocean or two between them. I don't know where Frosty was, all through that long day's ride; for me, I was back in little old Frisco, with Barney MacTague and the rest of the crowd; and part of the time, I know, I was telling dad what a mess he'd made of bringing up his only son.

That night we slept in a shack at the river - "Pochette Crossing" was the name it answered to - and shared the same bed. It was not remarkable for its comfort - that bed. I think the mattress was stuffed with potatoes; it felt that way.

Next morning we were off again, over the same bare, brown, unpeopled wilderness. Once we saw a badger zigzagging along a side-hill, and Frosty whipped out a big revolver - one of those "Colt 45's," I suppose - and shot it; he said in extenuation that they play the very devil with the range, digging holes for cow-punchers to break their necks over.

I was surprised at Frosty; there he had been armed, all the time, and I never guessed it. Even when we went to bed the night before, I had not glimpsed a weapon. Clearly, he could not be a cowboy, I reflected, else he would have worn a cartridge-belt sagging picturesquely down over one hip, and his gun dangling from it. He put the gun away, and I don't know where; somewhere out of sight it went, and Frosty turned off the trail and went driving wild across the prairie. I asked him why, and he said, "Short cut."

Then a wind crept out of the north, and with it the snow. We were climbing low ridges and dodging into hollows, and when the snow spread a white veil over the land, I looked at Frosty out of the tail of my eye, wondering if he did not wish he had kept to the road - trail, it is called in the rangeland.

If he did, he certainly kept it to himself; he went on climbing hills and setting the brake at the top, to slide into a hollow, and his face kept its inscrutable calm; whatever he thought was beyond guessing at.

When he had watered the horses at a little creek that was already skimmed with ice, and unwrapped a package of sandwiches on his knee and offered me one, I broke loose. Silence may be golden, but even old King Midas got too big a dose of gold, once upon a time, if one may believe tradition.

"I hate to butt into a man's meditations," I said, looking him straight in the eye, "but there's a limit to everything, and you've played right up to it. You've had time, my friend, to remember all your sins and plan enough more to keep you hustling the allotted span; you've been given an opportunity to reconstruct the universe and breed a new philosophy of life. For Heaven's sake, *say* something!"

Frosty eyed me for a minute, and the muscles at the corners of his mouth twitched. "Sure," he responded cheerfully. "I'm something like you; I hate to break into a man's meditations. It looks like snow."

"Do you think it's going to storm?" I retorted in the same tone; it had been snowing great guns for the last three hours. We both laughed, and Frosty unbent and told me a lot about Bay State Ranch and the country around it.

Part of the information was an eye-opener; I wished I had known it when dad was handing out that roast to me - I rather think I could have made him cry enough. I tagged the information and laid it away for future reference.

As I got the country mapped out in my mind, we were in a huge capital H. The eastern line, toward which we were angling, was a river they call the Midas - though I'll never tell you why, unless it's a term ironical. The western line is another river, the Joliette, and the cross-bar is a range of hills - they might almost be called mountains - which I had been facing all that morning till the snow came between and shut them off; White Divide, it is called, and we were creeping around the end, between them and the Midas. It seemed queer that there was no way of crossing, for the Bay State lies almost in a direct line south from Osage, Frosty told me, and the country we were traversing was rough as White Divide could be, and I said so to Frosty. Right here is where I got my first jolt.

"There's a fine pass cut through White Divide by old Mama Nature," Frosty said, in the sort of tone a man takes when he could say a lot more, but refrains.

"Then why in Heaven's name don't you travel it?"

"Because it isn't healthy for Ragged H folks to travel that way," he said, in the same eloquent tone.

"Who are the Ragged H folks, and what's the matter with them?" I wanted to know - for I smelled a mystery.

He looked at me sidelong. "If you didn't look just like the old man," he said, "I'd think yuh were a fake; the Ragged H is the brand your ranch is known by - the Bay State outfit. And it isn't healthy to travel King's Highway, because there's a large-sized feud between your father and old King. How does it happen yuh aren't wise to the family history?"

"Dad never unbosomed himself to me, that's why," I told him. "He has labored for twenty-five years under the impression that I was a kid just able to toddle alone. He didn't think he needed to tell me things; I know we've got a place called the Bay State Ranch somewhere in this part of the world, and I have reason to think I'm headed for it. That's about the extent of my knowledge of our interest here. I never heard of the White Divide before, or of this particular King. I'm thirsting for information."

"Well, it strikes me you've got it coming," said Frosty. "I always had your father sized up as being closed-mouthed, but I didn't think he made such a thorough job of it as all that. Old King has sure got it in for the Ragged H - or Bay State, if yuh'd rather call us that; and the Ragged H boys don't sit up nights thinking kind and loving thoughts about him, either. Thirty years ago your father and old King started jangling over water-rights, and I guess they burned powder a-plenty; King goes lame to this day from a bullet your old man planted in his left leg."

I dropped the flag and started him off again. "It's news to me,"

I put in, "and you can't tell me too much about it."

"Well," he said, "your old man was in the right of it; he owns all the land along Honey Creek, right up to White Divide, where it heads; uh course, he overlooked a bet there; he should have got a cinch on that pass, and on the head uh the creek. But he let her slide, and first he knew old King had come in and staked a claim and built him a shack right in our end of the pass, and camped down to stay. Your dad wasn't joyful. The Bay State had used that pass to trail herds through and as the easiest and shortest trail to the railroad; and then old King takes it up, strings a five-wired fence across at both ends of his place, and warns us off. I've heard Potter tell what warm times there were. Your father stayed right here and had it out with him. The Bay State was all he had, then, and he ran it himself. Perry Potter worked for him, and knows all about it. Neither old King nor your dad was married, and it's a wonder they didn't kill each other off - Potter says they sure tried. The time King got it in the leg your father and his punchers were coming home from a breed dance, and they were feeling pretty nifty, I guess; Potter told me they started out with six bottles, and when they got to White Divide there wasn't enough left to talk about. They cut King's fence at the north end, and went right through, hell-bent-for-election. King and his men boiled out, and they mixed good and plenty. Your father went home with a hole in his shoulder, and old King had one in his leg to match, and since then it's been war. They tried to fight it out in court, and King got the best of it there. Then they got married and kind o' cooled off, and pretty soon they both got so much stuff to look after that they didn't have much time to take pot-shots at each other, and now we're enjoying what yuh might call armed peace. We go round about sixty miles, and King's Highway is bad medicine.

"King owns the stage-line from Osage to Laurel, where the Bay State gets its mail, and he owns Kenmore, a mining-camp in the west half uh White Divide. We can go around by Kenmore, if we want to - but King's Highway? Nit!"

I chuckled to myself to think of all the things I could twit dad about if ever he went after me again. It struck me that I hadn't been a circumstance, so far, to what dad must have been in his youth. At my worst, I'd never shot a man.

CHAPTER III.

THE QUARREL RENEWED.

That night, by a close scratch, we made a little place Frosty said was one of the Bay State line-camps. I didn't know what a line-camp was, and it wasn't much for style, but it looked good to me, after riding nearly all day in a snow-storm. Frosty cooked dinner and I made the coffee, and we didn't have such a bad time of it, although the storm held us there for two days.

We sat by the little cook-stove and told yarns, and I pumped Frosty just about dry of all he'd ever heard about dad.

I hadn't intended to write to dad, but, after hearing all I did, I couldn't help handing out a gentle hint that I was on. When I'd been at the Bay State Ranch for a week, I wrote him a letter that, I felt, squared my account with him. It was so short that I can repeat every word now. I said:

DEAR DAD:

I am here. Though you sent me out here to reform me, I find the opportunities for unadulterated deviltry away ahead of Frisco. I saw our old neighbor, King, whom you may possibly remember. He still walks with a limp. By the way, dad, it seems to me that when you were about twenty-five you "indulged in some damned poor pastimes," yourself. Your dutiful son,

ELLIS.

B. M. BOWER

Dad never answered that letter.

Montana, as viewed from the Bay State Ranch in March, struck me as being an unholy mixture of brown, sodden hills and valleys, chill winds that never condescended to blow less than a gale, and dull, scurrying clouds, with sometimes a day of sunshine that was bright as our own sun at home. (You can't make me believe that our California sun bothers with any other country.)

I'd been used to a green world; I never would go to New York in the winter, because I hate the cold - and here I was, with the cold of New York and with none of the ameliorations in the way of clubs and theaters and the like. There were the hills along Midas River shutting off the East, and hills to the south that Frosty told me went on for miles and miles, and on the north stretched White Divide - only it was brown, and bleak, and several other undesirable things. When I looked at it, I used to wonder at men fighting over it. I did a heap of wondering, those first few days.

Taken in a lump, it wasn't my style, and I wasn't particular to keep my opinions a secret. For the ranch itself, it looked to me like a village of corrals and sheds and stables, evidently built with an eye to usefulness, and with the idea that harmony of outline is a sin and not to be tolerated. The house was put up on the same plan, gave shelter to Perry Potter and the cook, had a big, bare dining-room where the men all ate together without napkins or other accessories of civilization, and a couple of bedrooms that were colder, if I remember correctly, than outdoors. I know that the water froze in my pitcher the first night, and that afterward I performed my ablutions in the kitchen, and dipped hot water out of a tank with a blue dipper.

That first week I spent adjusting myself to the simple life, and trying to form an unprejudiced opinion of my companions in exile. As for the said companions, they sort of stood back and sized up my points, good and bad - and I've a notion they laid heavy odds against me, and had me down in the Also Ran bunch. I overheard one of them remark, when I was coming up from the stables: "Here's the son and heir - come, let's kill him!" Another one drawled: "What's the use? The bounty's run out."

I was convinced that they regarded me as a frost.

The same with Perry Potter, a grizzled little man with long, ragged beard and gray eyes that looked through you and away beyond. I had a feeling that dad had told him to keep an eye on me and report any incipient growth of horse-sense. I may have wronged him and dad, but that is how I felt, and I didn't like him any better for it. He left me alone, and I raised the bet and left him alone so hard that I scarcely exchanged three sentences with him in a week. The first night he asked after dad's health, and I told him the doctor wasn't making regular calls at the house. A day or so after he said: "How do you like the country?" I said: "Damn the country!" and closed *that* conversation. I don't remember that we had any more for awhile.

The cowboys were breaking horses to the saddle most of the time, for it was too early for round-up, I gathered. When I sat on the corral fence and watched the fun, I observed that I usually had my rail all to myself and that the rest of the audience roosted somewhere else. Frosty Miller talked with me sometimes, without appearing to suffer any great pain, but Frosty was always the star actor when the curtain rose on a bronco-breaking act. As for the rest, they made it plain that I did *not* belong to their set, and I wasn't sending them my At Home cards, either. We were as haughty with each other as two society matrons when each aspires to be called leader.

Then a blizzard that lasted five days came ripping down over that desolation, and everybody stuck close to shelter, and amused themselves as they could. The cowboys played cards most of the time - seven-up, or pitch, or poker; they didn't ask me to take a hand, though; I fancy they were under the impression that I didn't know how to play.

I never was much for reading; it's too slow and tame. I'd much rather get out and *live* the story I like best. And there was nothing to read, anyway. I went rummaging in my trunks, and in the bottom of one I came across a punching-bag and a set of gloves. Right there I took off my hat to Rankin, and begged his pardon for the unflattering names he'd been in the habit of hearing from me. I carried the things down and put up the bag in an empty room at one end of the bunk-house, and got busy.

Frosty Miller came first to see what was up, and I got him to put on the gloves for awhile; he knew something of the manly art, I discovered, and we went at it fast and furious. I think I broke up a game in the next room. The boys came to the door, one by one, and stood watching, until we had the full dozen for audience. Before any one realized what was happening, we were playing together real pretty, with the chilly shoulder barred and the social ice gone the way of a dew-drop in the sun.

We boxed and wrestled, with much scientific discussion of "full Nelsons" and the like, and even fenced with sticks. I had them going there, and could teach them things; and they were the willingest pupils a man ever had - docile and filled with a deep respect for their teacher who knew all there was to know - or, if he didn't, he never let on. Before night we had smashed three window-panes, trimmed several faces down considerably, and got pretty well acquainted. I found out that they weren't so far behind the old gang at home for wanting all there is in the way of fun, and I believe they discovered that I was harmless. Before that storm let up they were dealing cards to me, and allowing me to get rid of the rest of the forty dollars Rankin had overlooked. I got some of it back.

I went down and bunked with them, because they had a stove and I didn't, and it was more sociable; Perry Potter and the cook were welcome to the house, I told them, except at meal-times. And, more than all the rest, I could keep out of range of

Perry Potter's eyes. I never could get used to that watch-Willie-grow way he had, or rid myself of the notion that he was sending dad a daily report of my behavior.

The next thing, when the weather quit sifting snow and turned on the balmy breezes and the sunshine, I was down in the corrals in my chaps and spurs, learning things about horses that I never suspected before. When I did something unusually foolish, the boys were good enough to remember my boxing and fencing and such little accomplishments, and did not withdraw their favor; so I went on, butting into every new game that came up, and taking all bets regardless, and actually began to wise up a little and to forget a few of my grievances.

I was down in the corral one day, saddling Shylock - so named because he tried to exact a pound of flesh every time I turned my back or in other ways seemed off my guard - and when I was looping up the latigo I discovered that the alliterative Mr. Potter was roosting on the fence, watching me with those needle-pointed eyes of his. I wondered if he was about to prepare another report for dad.

"Do yuh want to be put on the pay-roll?" he asked, without any preamble, when he caught my glance.

"Yes, if I'm *earning* wages. 'The laborer is worthy of his hire,' I believe," I retorted loftily. The fact was, I was strapped again - and, though one did not need money on the Bay State Ranch, it's a good thing to have around.

He grinned into his collar. "Well," he said, "you've been pretty busy the last three weeks, but I ain't had any orders to hire a boxing-master for the boys. I don't know as that'd rightly come under the head of legitimate expenses; boxing-masters come high, I've heard. Are yuh going on round-up?"

"Sure!" I answered, in an exact copy - as near as I could make it - of Frosty Miller's intonation. I was making Frosty my model those days.

He said: "All right - your pay starts on the fifteenth of next month" - which was April. Then he got down from the fence and went off, and I mounted Shylock and rode away to Laurel, after the mail. Not that I expected any, for no one but dad knew where I was, and I hadn't heard a word from him, though I knew he wrote to Perry Potter - or his secretary did - every week or so. Really, I don't think a father ought to be so chesty with the only son he's got, even if the son is a no-account young cub.

I was standing in the post-office, which was a store and saloon as well, when an old fellow with stubby whiskers and a jaw that looked as though it had been trimmed square with a rule, and a limp that made me know at once who he was, came in. He was standing at the little square window, talking to the postmaster and waving his pipe to emphasize what he said, when a horse went past the door on the dead run, with bridle-reins flying. A fellow rushed out past us - it was his horse - and hit old King's elbow a clip as he went by. The pipe went about ten feet and landed in a pickle-keg. I went after it and fished it out for the old fellow - not so much because I'm filled with a natural courtesy, as because I was curious to know the man that had got the best of dad.

He thanked me, and asked me across to the saloon side of the room to drink with him. "I don't know as I've met you before, young man," he said, eying me puzzled. "Your face is familiar, though; been in this country long?"

"No," I said; "a little over a month is all."

"Well, if you ever happen around my way - King's Highway, they call my place - stop and see me. Going to stay long out here?"

"I think so," I replied, motioning the waiter - "bar-slave," they call them in Montana - to refill our glasses. "And I'll be glad to call some day, when I happen in your neighborhood. And if you ever ride over toward the Bay State, be sure you stop."

Well, say! old King turned the color of a ripe prune; every hair in that stubble of beard stood straight out from his chin, and he looked as if murder would be a pleasant thing. He took the glass and deliberately emptied the whisky on the floor. "John Carleton's son, eh? I might 'a' known it - yuh look enough like him. Me drink with a son of John Carleton? That breed uh wolves had better not come howling around *my* door. I asked yuh to come t' King's Highway, young man, and I don't take it back. You can come, but you'll get the same sort uh welcome I'd give that -"

Right there I got my hand on his throttle. He was an old man, comparatively, and I didn't want to hurt him; but no man under heaven can call my dad the names he did, and I told him so. "I don't want to dig up that old quarrel, King," I said, shaking him a bit with one hand, just to emphasize my words, "but you've got to speak civilly of dad, or, by the Lord! I'll turn you across my knee and administer a stinging rebuke."

He tried to squirm loose, and to reach behind him with that suggestive movement that breeds trouble among men of the plains; but I held his arms so he couldn't move, the while I told him a lot of things about true politeness - things that I wasn't living up to worth mentioning. He yelled to the postmaster to grab me, and the fellow tried it. I backed into a corner and held old King in front of me as a bulwark, warranted bullet proof, and wondered what kind of a hornet's-nest I'd got into. The waiter and the postmaster were both looking for an opening, and I remembered that I was on old King's territory, and that they were after holding their jobs.

I don't know how it would have ended - I suppose they'd have got me, eventually - but Perry Potter walked in, and it didn't seem to take him all day to savvy the situation. He whipped out a gun and leveled it at the enemy, and told me to scoot and get on my horse.

"Scoot nothing!" I yelled back. "What about you in the meantime? Do you think I'm going to leave them to clean you up?"

He smiled sourly at me. "I've held my own with this bunch uh trouble-hunters for thirty years," he said dryly. "I guess yuh ain't got any reason t' be alarmed. Come out uh that corner and let 'em alone."

I don't, to this day, know why I did it, but I quit hugging old King, and the other two fell back and gave me a clear path to the door. "King was blackguarding dad, and I couldn't stand for it," I explained to Perry Potter as I went by. "If you're not going, I won't."

"I've got a letter to mail," he said, calm as if he were in his own corral. "You went off before I got a chance to give it to yuh. I'll be out in a minute."

He went and slipped the letter into the mail-box, turned his back on the three, and walked out as if nothing had happened; perhaps he knew that I was watching them, in a mood to do things if they offered to touch him. But they didn't, and we mounted our horses and rode away, and Perry Potter never mentioned the affair to me, then or after. I don't think we spoke on the way to the ranch; I was busy wishing I'd been around in that part of the world thirty years before, and thinking what a lot of fun I had missed by not being as old as dad. A quarrel thirty years old is either mighty stale and unprofitable, or else, like wine, it improves with age. I meant to ride over to King's Highway some day, and see how he would have welcomed dad thirty years before.

CHAPTER IV.

THROUGH KING'S HIGHWAY.

It was a long time before I was in a position to gratify my curiosity, though; between the son and heir, with nothing to do but amuse himself, and a cowboy working for his daily wage, there is a great gulf fixed. After being put on the pay-roll, I couldn't do just as my fancy prompted. I had to get up at an ungodly hour, and eat breakfast in about two minutes, and saddle a horse and "ride circle" with the rest of them – which same is exceeding wearisome to man and beast. For the first time since I left school, I was under orders; and the foreman certainly tried to obey dad's mandate and treat me just as he would have treated any other stranger. I could give it up, of course - but I hope never to see the day when I can be justly called a quitter.

First, we were rounding up horses - saddlers that were to be ridden in the round-up proper. We were not more than two or three weeks at that, though we covered a good deal of country. Before it was over I knew a lot more than when we started out, and had got hard as nails; riding on round-up beats a gym for putting wire muscles under a man's skin, in my opinion. We worked all around White Divide - which was turning a pale, dainty green except where the sandstone cliffs stood up in all the shades of yellow and red. Montana, as viewed on "horse round-up," looks better than in the first bleak days of March, and I could gaze upon it without profanity. I even got to like tearing over the newborn grass on a good horse, with a cowboy or two galloping, keen-faced and calm, beside me. It was almost better than slithering along a hard road with a motor-car stripped to the running-gear.

When the real thing happened - the "calf round-up" - and thirty riders in white felt hats, chaps, spurs a-jingle, and handkerchief ends flying out in the wind, lined up of a morning for orders, the blood of me went a-jump, and my nerves were all tingly with the pure joy of being alive and atop a horse as eager as hounds in the leash and with the wind of the plains in my face and the grass-land lying all around, yelling come on, and the meadowlarks singing fit to split their throats. There's nothing like it - and I've tried nearly everything in the way of blood-tinglers. Skimming through the waves, alean to the wind in a racing-yacht, comes nearest, and even that takes second money when circle-riding on round-up is entered in the race. But this is getting away from my story.

We were working the country just north of White Divide, when the foreman started me home with a message for Perry Potter - and I was to get back as soon as possible with the answer. Now, here's where I got gay.

As I said, we were north of White Divide, and the home ranch was south, and to go around either end of that string of hills meant an extra sixty miles to cover each way - a hundred and twenty for the round trip. Directly in the way of the proverbial crow's flight lay King's Highway, which - if I got through - would put me at the ranch the first day, and back at camp the second; and I rather guessed that would surprise our worthy foreman not a little. I didn't see why it couldn't be done; surely old King wouldn't murder a man just for riding through that pass - that would be bloody-minded indeed!

And if I failed - why, I could go around, and no one would be wise to the fact that I had tried it. I headed straight for the pass, which yawned invitingly, with two bare peaks for the jaws, not over six miles away. It was against orders, for Perry Potter had given the boys to understand that they were not to go that way, and that they were to leave King and his stronghold strictly alone; but I didn't worry about that. When I was fairly in the mouth of the pass, I got down and looked to the cinch, and then rode boldly forward, like a soldier riding up to the cannon's mouth with a smile on his face. Oh, I wasted plenty of admiration on one Ellis Carleton about that time, and rehearsed the bold, biting speech I meant to deliver at old King's very door.

So far it was easy sailing. There was a hard-beaten road, and the hills seemed standing back and holding aside their skirts for a free passing. The sun lay warm on their green slopes, and one could fairly smell the grass growing. In the hollows were worlds of blue flowers, with patches here and there a royal purple. I stopped and gathered a handful and stuck them in my buttonhole and under my hatband. I don't know when I have felt so thoroughly satisfied with said Ellis Carleton - of whom I am overfond of speaking - I even mimicked the meadow-larks, until they watched me with heads tilted, not knowing what to make of such an impertinent fellow.

King's Highway was glorious; I didn't wonder that dad thought it worth fighting over, and as I went on, farther and farther down this lane made by nature for easy passing, I could see what an immense advantage it would be to take herds through that way. I could see why the Bay State men cursed King when they took the rough trail around the end of White Divide.

After an hour of undisputed riding on this forbidden trail, the pass narrowed rather abruptly till it was not more than a furlong in width; the hills stretched their heads still higher, as if they wanted to see the fun, and the shadow of the eastern rim laid clear across the narrow valley and touched the foot of the opposite slope. I hope I am not going to be called nervous if I tell the truth about things; when I rode into the shadow I stopped whistling a bad imitation of meadow-lark notes. A bit farther and I pulled up, looked all around, and got off and tightened the cinch a bit more. Shylock - I always rode him when I could - threw his head around and nearly took a chunk out of my arm, and in reproving him I forgot, for a minute, the ticklish game I was playing. Then I loosened my gun - I had learned to carry it inconspicuously under my coat, as did the other boys - made sure it could be pulled without embarrassing delay, and went on. Around the next turn a five-wired fence stretched across the trail, with a gate fastened by a chain and padlock. I whistled under my breath, and eyed the lock with extreme disfavor.

But I had learned a trick of the cowboys. I pulled the wire off a couple of posts at one side of the gate, laid them flat on the ground, and led Shylock over them. Then I found a rock, pounded the staples back in place, and went on; only for the tracks, one could not notice that any had passed that way. Still, it was a bit ticklish, riding down King's Highway alone and with no idea of what lay farther on. But dad had dared go that way, and to fight at the far end; and what dad had not been afraid to tackle, it did not behoove his son to back down from. I made Shylock walk the next half-mile, with some notion of saving his wind for an emergency run.

Of a sudden I rounded a sharp nose of hill and came plump on the palace of the King. It looked a good deal like the Bay State Ranch - big corrals and sheds and stables, and little place for man to dwell. The house, though, was bigger than ours, and looked more comfortable to live in. And the thing that struck me most was the head which King displayed for strategy. The trail wound between those same sheds and corrals, a gantlet two hundred yards long that one must run or turn back. On either side the bluffs rose sheer, with the buildings crowding close against their base. I didn't wonder Frosty called King's Highway "bad medicine." It certainly did look like it.

I went softly along that trail, turning sharp corners around a shed here, circling a corral there, with my hand within an inch of my gun, and my heart within an inch of my teeth, and you may laugh all you like.

No one seemed to be about; the sheds were deserted, and a few horses dozed in a corral that I passed; but human being I saw none. It was evident that King did not consider his enemy worth watching. I passed the last shed and found myself headed straight for the house; I had still to get through its very dooryard before I was in any position to crow, and beyond the house was another fence; I hoped the gate was not locked. Shylock pricked up his ears, then laid them back along his neck as if he did not approve the layout, either. But we ambled right along, like a deacon headed for prayer-meeting, and I tried to look in four different directions at one and the same time.

For that reason, I didn't see her till she stood right in front of me; and when I did, I stared like an idiot. It was a girl, and she was coming down a path to the trail, with her hands full of flowers, for all the world like a Duchess novel. Another minute, and I'd have run over her, I guess. She stopped and looked at me from under lashes so thick and heavy they seemed almost pulling her lids shut, and there was something in her eyes that made me go hot and cold, like I was coming down with grippe; when she spoke my symptoms grew worse.

"Did you wish to see father?" she asked, as if she were telling me to leave the place.

"I believe," I rallied enough to answer, "that 'father' would give a good deal to see *me*." Then that seemed to shut off our conversation too abruptly to suit me; there are occasions when prickly chills have a horrible fascination for a fellow; this was one of the times.

"He's not at home, I'm very sorry to say," she retorted in the same liquid-air voice as before, and turned to go back to the house.

I thanked the Lord for that, in a whisper, and kept pace with her. It was plain she hated the sight of me, but I counted on her being enough like her dad not to run away.

"May I trouble you for a drink of water?" I asked, in the orthodox tone of humility.

"There is no need to trouble me; there is the creek, beyond the house; you are welcome to all you want."

"Thanks." I watched the pink curve of her cheek, and knew she was dying for a chance to snub me still more maliciously. We were at the steps of the veranda now, but still she would not hurry; she seemed to hate even the semblance of running away.

"Can you direct me to the Bay State Ranch?" I hazarded. It was my last card, and I let it go with a sigh.

She pointed a slim, scornful finger at the brand on Shylock's shoulder.

"If you are in doubt of the way, Mr. Carleton, your horse will take you home - if you give him his head."

That put a crimp in me worse than the look of her eyes, even. I stared at her a minute, and then laughed right out. "The game's yours, Miss King, and I take off my hat to you for hitting straight and hard," I said. "Must the feud descend even to the second generation? Is it a fight to the finish, and no quarter asked or given?"

I had her going then. She blushed - and when I saw the red creep into her cheeks my heart was hardened to repentance. I'd have done it again for the pleasure of seeing her that way.

"You are taking a good deal for granted, sir," she said, in her loftiest tone. "We Kings scarcely consider the Carletons worthy our weapons."

"You don't, eh? Then, why did you begin it?" I wanted to know. "If you permit me, you started the row before I spoke, even."

"I do *not* permit you." Clearly, my lady could be haughty enough to satisfy the most fastidious.

"Well," I sighed, "I will go my way. I'm a lover of peace, myself; but since you proclaim war, war it must be. I'm not so ungallant as to oppose a lady's wishes. Is that gate down there locked?"

"Figuratively, it's *always* locked against the Carletons," she said.

"But I want to go through it *literally*," I retorted. And she just looked at me from under those lashes, and never answered.

"Well, the air grows chill in King's Highway," I shivered mockingly. "If ever I find you on Bay State soil, Miss King, I shall take much pleasure in teaching you the proper way to treat an enemy."

"I shall be greatly diverted, no doubt," was the scornful reply of her - and just then an old lady came to the door, and I lifted my hand grandly in a precise military salute and rode away, wondering which of us had had the best of it.

The gate wasn't locked, and as for taking a drink at the creek, I forgot that I was thirsty. I jogged along toward home, and wondered why Frosty had not told me that King had a daughter. Also, I wondered at her animosity. It never occurred to me that her father, unlike my dad, had probably harped on the Carletons until she had come to think we were in league with the Old Boy himself. Her dad's game leg would no doubt argue strongly against us, and keep the feud green in her heart - supposing she had one.

On the whole, I was glad I had traveled King's Highway. I had discovered a brand-new enemy - and so far in my life enemies had been so scarce as to be a positive diversion. And it was novel and interesting to be so thoroughly hated by a girl. No reason to dodge *her* net. I rather congratulated myself on knowing one girl who positively refused to smile on demand. She hadn't, once. I got to wondering, that night, if she had dimples. I meant to find out.

CHAPTER V.

INTO THE LION'S MOUTH.

Perry Potter, when he had read the foreman's note, asked how long since I left camp; when I told him that I was there at daylight, he looked at me queerly and walked off without a word. I didn't say anything, either.

I stayed at the ranch overnight, intending to start back the next morning. The round-up would be west of where I had left them, according to the foreman - or wagon-boss, as he is called. Logically, then, I should take the trail that led through Kenmore, the mining-camp owned by King, and which lay in the heart of White Divide ten miles west of King's Highway. That, I say, was the logical route - but I wasn't going to take it. I wasn't a bit stuck on that huddle of corrals and sheds, with the trail winding blindly between, and I wasn't in love with the girl or with old King; but, all the same, I meant to go back the way I came, just for my own private satisfaction.

While I was saddling Shylock, in the opal-tinted sunrise, Potter came down and gave me the letter to the wagon-boss, an answer to the one I had brought.

"Here's some chuck the cook put up for yuh," he remarked, handing me a bundle tied up in a flour-sack. "You'll need it 'fore yuh get through to camp; you'll likely be longer going than yuh was comin'."

"Think so?" I smiled knowingly to myself and left him staring disapprovingly after me. I could easily give a straight guess at what he was thinking.

I jogged along as leisurely as I could without fretting Shylock, and, once clear of the home field, headed straight for King's Highway. It wasn't the wisest course I could take, perhaps, but it was like to prove the most exciting, and I never was remarkable for my wisdom. It seemed to me that it was necessary to my self-respect to return the way I came - and I may as well confess that I hoped Miss King was an early riser. As it was, I killed what time I could, and so spent a couple of hours where one would have sufficed.

Half a mile out from the mouth of the pass, I observed a human form crowning the peak of a sharp-pointed little butte that rose up out of the prairie; since the form seemed to be in skirts, I made for the spot. Shylock puffed up the steep slope, and at last stopped still and looked back at me in utter disgust; so I took the hint and got off, and led him up the rest of the way.

"Good morning. We meet on neutral ground," I greeted when I was close behind her. "I propose a truce."

She jumped a bit, and looked very much astonished to see me there so close. If it had been some other girl - say Ethel Mapleton - I'd have suspected the genuineness of that surprise; as it was, I could only think she had been very much absorbed not to hear me scrambling up there.

"You're an early bird," she said dryly, "to be so far from home." She glanced toward the pass, as though she would like to cut and run, but hated to give me the satisfaction.

"Well," I told her with inane complacency, "you will remember that 'it's the early bird that catches the worm.'"

"What a pretty speech!" she commented, and I saw what I'd

done, and felt myself turn a beautiful purple. Compare her to a worm!

But she laughed when she saw how uncomfortable I was, and after that I was almost glad I'd said it; she *did* have dimples - two of them - and -

The laugh, however, was no sign of incipient amiability, as I very soon discovered. She turned her back on me and went imperturbably on with her sketching; she was trying to put on paper the lights and shades of White Divide - and even a desire to be chivalrous will not permit me to lie and say that she was making any great success of it. I don't believe the Lord ever intended her for an artist.

"Aren't you giving King's Highway a much wider mouth than it's entitled to?" I asked mildly, after watching her for a minute.

"I should not be surprised," she told me haughtily, "if you some day wished it still wider."

"There wouldn't be the chance for fighting, if it was; and I take great pleasure in keeping the feud going."

"I thought you were anxious for a truce," she said recklessly, shading a slope so that it looked like the peak of a roof.

"I am," I retorted shamelessly. "I'm anxious for anything under the sun that will keep you talking to me. People might call that a flirtatious remark, but I plead not guilty; I wouldn't know how to flirt, even if I wanted to do so."

She turned her head and looked at me in a way that I could not misunderstand; it was plain, unvarnished scorn, and a ladylike anger, and a few other unpleasant things.

It made me think of a certain star in "The Taming of the Shrew."

B. M. BOWER

"Fie, fie! unknit that threatening, unkind brow,
And dart not scornful glances from those eyes,
To wound thy neighbor and thine enemy,"

I declaimed, with rather a free adaptation to my own need.

Her brow positively refused to unknit. "Have you nothing to do but spout bad quotations from Shakespeare on a hilltop?" she wanted to know, in a particularly disagreeable tone.

"Plenty; I have yet to win that narrow pass," I said.

"Hardly to-day," she told me, with more than a shade of triumph. "Father is at home, and he heard of your trip yesterday."

If she expected to scare me by that! "Must our feud include your father? When I met him a month ago, he gave me a cordial invitation to stop, if I ever happened this way."

She lifted those heavy lashes, and her eyes plainly spoke unbelief.

"It's a fact," I assured her calmly. "I met him one day in Laurel, and was fortunate enough to perform a service which earned his gratitude. As I say, he invited me to come and see him; I told him I should be glad to have him visit me at the Bay State Ranch, and we embraced each other with much fervor."

"Indeed!" I could see that she persisted in doubting my veracity.

"Ask your father if we didn't," I said, much injured. I knew she wouldn't, though.

A scrambling behind us made me turn, and there was Perry Potter climbing up to us, his eyes sharper than ever, and his face so absolutely devoid of expression that it told me a good deal. I'll lay all I own he was a good bit astonished at what he saw! As for me, I could have kicked him back to the bottom of the hill - and I probably looked it.

"There was something I forgot to put in that note," he said evenly, just touching the brim of his hat in acknowledgment of the girl's presence. "I wrote another one. I'd like Ballard to get it as soon as you can make camp - conveniently." His eyes looked through me almost as if I weren't there.

My desire to kick him grew almost into mania. I took the note, saw at a glance that it was addressed to me, and said: "All right," in a tone quite different from the one I had been using to tease Miss King.

He gave me another sharp look, and went back the way he had come, leaving me standing there glaring after him. Miss King, I noticed, was sketching for dear life, and her cheeks were crimson.

When Potter had got to the bottom and was riding away, I unfolded the note and read:

> Don't be a fool. For God's sake, have some sense and keep away from King's Highway.

I laughed, and Miss King looked up inquiringly. Following an impulse I've never yet been able to classify, I showed her the note.

She read it calmly - I might say indifferently. "He is quite right," she said coldly. "I, too - if I cared enough - would advise you to keep away from King's Highway."

"But you don't care enough to advise me, and so I shall go," I said - and I had the satisfaction of seeing her teeth come down sharply on her lower lip. I waited a minute, watching her.

"You're very foolish," she said icily, and went at her sketching again.

I waited another minute; during that time she succeeded in making the pass look weird indeed, and a fearsome place to enter. I got reckless.

"You've spoiled that sketch," I said, stooping and taking it gently from her. "Give it to me, and it shall be a flag of truce with which I shall win my way through unscathed."

She started to her feet then, and her anger was worth facing for the glow it brought to eyes and cheeks, and the tremble that came to her lips.

"Mr. Carleton, you are perfectly detestable!" she cried.

"Miss King, you are perfectly adorable!" I returned, folding the sketch very carefully, so that it would slip easily into my pocket. "With so authentic a map of the enemy's stronghold, what need I fear? I go - but, on my honor, I shall shortly return."

She stood with her fingers clasped tightly in front of her, and watched me lead Shylock down that butte - on the side toward the pass, if you are still in doubt of my intentions. When I say she watched me, I am making a guess; but I felt that she was, and it would be hard to disabuse my mind of that belief. And when I started, her fingers had been clinging tightly together. At the bottom I turned and waved my hat - and I know she saw that, for she immediately whirled and took to studying the southern sky-line. So I left her and galloped straight into the lion's den - to use an old simile.

I passed through the gate and up to the house, Shylock pacing easily along as though we both felt assured of a welcome. Old King met me at his door as I was going by; I pulled up and gave him my very cheeriest good morning. He looked at me from under shaggy, gray eyebrows.

"You've got your gall, young man, to come this way twice in twenty-four hours," he said grimly.

"You can turn around and go back the way you came in."

"You asked me to call," I reminded him mildly. "You were not at home yesterday, so I came again."

He glanced uneasily over his shoulder, and drew the door shut between himself and whoever was within. "You damn' cur," he growled, "yuh know yuh ain't no friend uh the Kings."

"I know you're all mighty unneighborly," I said, making me a cigarette in the way that cowboys do. "I asked a young lady - your daughter, I suppose - for a drink of water. She told me to go to the creek."

He laughed at that; evidently he approved of his daughter's attitude. "Beryl knows how to deal with the likes uh you," he muttered relishfully. "And she hates the Carletons bad as I do. Get off my place, young man, and do it quick!"

"Sure!" I assented cheerfully, and jabbed the spurs into Shylock - taking good care that he was beaded north instead of south. And it's a fact that, ticklish as was the situation, my first thought was: "So her name's Beryl, is it? Mighty pretty name, and fits her, too."

King wasn't thinking anything so sentimental, I'll wager. He yelled to two or three fellows, as I shot by them near the first corral: "Round up that thus-and-how" - I hate to say the words right out - "and bring him back here!" Then he sent a bullet zipping past my ear, and from the house came a high, nasal squawk which, I gathered, came from the old party I had seen the day before.

I went clippety-clip around those sheds and corrals, till I like to have snapped my head off; I knew Shylock could take first money over any ordinary cayuse, and I let him out; but, for all that, I heard them coming, and it sounded as if they were about to ride all over me, they were so close.

Past the last shed I went streaking it, and my heart remembered what it was made for, and went to work. I don't feel that, under the circumstances, it's any disgrace to own that I was scared. I didn't hear any more little singing birds fly past, so I straightened up enough to look around and see what was doing in the way of pursuit.

One glance convinced me that my pursuers weren't going to sleep in their saddles. One of them, on a little buckskin that was running with his ears laid so flat it looked as if he hadn't any, was widening the loop in his rope, and yelling unfriendly things as he spurred after me; the others were a length behind, and I mentally put them out of the race. The gentleman with the businesslike air was all I wanted to see, and I laid low as I could and slapped Shylock along the neck, and told him to bestir himself.

He did. We skimmed up that trail like a winner on the home – stretch , and before I had time to think of what lay ahead, I saw that fence with the high, board gate that was padlocked. Right there I swore abominably - but it didn't loosen the gate. I looked back and decided that this was no occasion for pulling wires loose and leading my horse over them. It was no occasion for anything that required more than a second; my friend of the rope was not more than five long jumps behind, and he was swinging that loop suggestively over his head.

I reined Shylock sharply out of the trail, saw a place where the fence looked a bit lower than the average, and put him straight at it with quirt and spurs. He would have swung off, but I've ridden to hounds, and I had seen hunters go over worse places; I held him to it without mercy. He laid back his ears, then, and went over - and his hind feet caught the top wire and snapped it like thread. I heard it hum through the air, and I heard those behind me shout as though something unlooked-for had happened. I turned, saw them gathered on the other side looking after me blankly, and I waved my hat airily in farewell and went on about my business.

I felt that they would scarcely chase me the whole twelve or fifteen miles of the pass, and I was right; after I turned the first bend I saw them no more.

At camp I was received with much astonishment, particularly when Ballard saw that I had brought an answer to his note.

"Yuh must 'a' rode King's Highway," he said, looking at me much as Perry Potter had done the night before.

I told him I did, and the boys gathered round and wanted to know how I did it. I told them about jumping the fence, and my conceit got a hard blow there; with one accord they made it plain that I had done a very foolish thing. Range horses, they assured me, are not much at jumping, as a rule; and wire-fences are their special abhorrence. Frosty Miller told me, in confidence, that he didn't know which was the bigger fool, Shylock or me, and he hoped I'd never be guilty of another trick like that.

That rather took the bloom off my adventure, and I decided, after much thought, that I agreed with Frosty: King's Highway was bad medicine. I amended that a bit, and excepted Beryl King; I did not think she was "bad medicine," however acid might be her flavor.

CHAPTER VI.

I ASK BERYL KING TO DANCE.

If I were just yarning for the fun there is in it, I should say that I was back in King's Highway, helping Beryl King gather posies and brush up her repartee, the very next morning - or the second, at the very latest. As a matter of fact, though, I steered clear of that pass, and behaved myself and stuck to work for six long weeks; that isn't saying I never thought about her, though.

On the very last day of June, as nearly as I could estimate, Frosty rode into Kenmore for something, and came back with that in his eyes that boded mischief; his words, however, were innocent enough for the most straight-laced.

"There's things doing in Kenmore," he remarked to a lot of us. "Old King has a party of aristocrats out from New York, visiting - Terence Weaver, half-owner in the mines, and some women; they're fixing to celebrate the Fourth with a dance. The women, it seems, are crazy to see a real Montana dance, and watch the cowboys *chasse* around the room in their chaps and spurs and big hats, and with two or three six-guns festooned around their middles, the way you see them in pictures. They think, as near as I could find out, that cowboys always go to dances in full war-paint like that - and they'll be disappointed if said cowboys don't punctuate the performance by shooting out the lights, every so often." He looked across at me, and then is when I observed the mischief brewing in his eyes.

"We'll have to take it in," I said promptly. "I'm anxious to see a Montana dance, myself."

"We aren't in their set," gloomed Frosty, with diplomatic caution. "I won't swear they're sending out engraved invitations, but, all the same, we won't be expected."

"We'll go, anyhow," I answered boldly. "If they want to see cow-punchers, it seems to me the Ragged H can enter a bunch that will take first prize."

Frosty looked at me, and permitted himself to smile. "Uh course, if you're bound to go, Ellis, I guess there's no stopping yuh - and some of us will naturally have to go along to see yuh through. King's minions would sure do things to yuh if yuh went without a body-guard." He shook his head, and cupped his hands around a match-blaze and a cigarette, so that no one could tell much about his expression.

"I'm bound to go," I declared, taking the cue. "And I think I do need some of you to back me up. I think," I added judicially, "I shall need the whole bunch."

The "bunch" looked at one another gravely and sighed. "We'll have t' go, I reckon," they said, just as though they weren't dying to play the unexpected guest. So that was decided, and there was much whispering among groups when they thought the wagon-boss was near, and much unobtrusive preparation.

It happened that the wagons pulled in close to the ranch the day before the Fourth, intending to lay over for a day or so. We were mighty glad of it, and hurried through our work. I don't know why the rest were so anxious to attend that dance, but for me, I'm willing to own that I wanted to see Beryl King. I knew she'd be there - and if I didn't manage, by fair means or foul, to make her dance with me, I should be very much surprised and disappointed. I couldn't remember ever giving so much thought to a girl; but I suppose it was because she was so frankly antagonistic that there was nothing tame about our intercourse. I can't like girls who invariably say just what you expect them to say.

When we came to get ready, there was a dress-discussion that a lot of women would find it hard to beat. Some of the boys wanted to play up to, the aristocrats' expectations, and wear their gaudiest neckerchiefs, their chaps, spurs, and all the guns they could get their hands on; but I had an idea I thought beat theirs, and proselyted for all I was worth. Rankin had packed a lot of dress suits in one of my trunks - evidently he thought Montana was some sort of house-party - and I wanted to build a surprise for the good people at King's. I wanted the boys to use those suits to the best advantage.

At first they hung back. They didn't much like the idea of wearing borrowed clothes - which attitude I respected, but felt bound to overrule. I told them it was no worse than borrowing guns, which a lot of them were doing. In the end my oratory was rewarded as it deserved; it was decided that, as even my capacious trunks couldn't be expected to hold thirty dress suits, part of the crowd should ride in full regalia. I might "tog up" as many as possible, and said "togged" men must lend their guns to the others; for every man of the "reals" insisted on wearing a gun dangling over each hip.

So I went down into my trunks, and disinterred four dress suits and three Tuxedos, together with all the appurtenances thereto. Oh, Rankin was certainly a wonder! There was a gay-colored smoking-jacket and cap that one of the boys took a fancy to and insisted on wearing, but I drew the line at that. We nearly had a fight over it, right there.

When we were dressed - and I had to valet the whole lot of them, except Frosty, who seemed wise to polite apparel - we were certainly a bunch of winners. Modesty forbids explaining just how *I* appear in a dress suit. I will only say that my tailor knew his business - but the others were fearful and wonderful to look upon. To begin with, not all of them stand six-feet-one in their stocking-feet, or tip the scales at a hundred and eighty odd; likewise their shoulders lacked the breadth that goes with the other measurements. Hence my tailor would doubtless have wept at the sight; shoulders drooping spiritlessly, and sleeves turned up, and trousers likewise. Frosty Miller, though, was like a man with his mask off; he stood there looking the gentleman born, and I couldn't help staring at him.

"You've been broken to society harness, old man, and are bridle-wise," I said, slapping him on the shoulder. He whirled on me savagely, and his face was paler than I'd ever seen it.

"And if I have - what the hell is it to you?" he asked unpleasantly, and I stammered out some kind of apology. Far be it from me to pry into a man's past.

I straightened Sandy Johnson's tie, turned up his sleeves another inch, and we started out. And I will say we were a quaint-looking outfit. Perhaps my meaning will be clearer when I say that every one of us wore the soft, white "Stetson" of the range-land, and a silk handkerchief knotted loosely around the throat, and spurs and riding-gloves. I've often wondered if the range has ever seen just that wedding of the East and the West before in man's apparel.

We'd scarcely got started when the wind caught Frosty's coat-tails and slapped them down along the flanks of his horse - an incident that the horse met with stern disapproval. He went straight up into the air, and then bucked as long as his wind held out, the while Frosty's quirt kept time with the tails of his coat.

When the two had calmed down a bit, the other boys profited by Frosty's experience, and tucked the coat-tails snugly under them - and those who wore the Tuxedos congratulated themselves on their foresight. We were a merry party, and we were willing to publish the fact.

When we had overtaken the others we were still merrier, for the spectacular contingent plumed themselves like peacocks on their fearsomeness, and guyed us conventionally garbed fellows unmercifully.

When the thirty of us filed into the long, barn-like hall where they were having the dance, I believe I can truthfully say that we created a sensation. That "ripple of excitement" which we read about so often in connection with belles and balls went round the room. Frosty and I led the way, and the rest of the "biscuit-shooter brigade," as the others called us, followed two by two. Then came the real Wild West show, with their hats tilted far back on their heads and brazen faces which it pained me to contemplate. We arrived during that humming hash which comes just after a number, and every one stared impolitely, and some of them not overcordially. I began to wonder if we hadn't done a rather ill-bred thing, to hurl ourselves so unceremoniously into the merrymakings of the enemy; but I comforted myself with the thought that the dance was given as a public affair, so that we were acting within our technical rights - though I own that, as I looked around upon our crowd, ranged solemnly along the wall, it struck me that we *were* a bit spectacular.

She was there, chatting with some other women, at the far end of the hall, and if she saw me enter the room she did not show any disquietude; from where I stood, she seemed perfectly at ease, and unconscious of anything unusual having occurred. Old King I could not see.

A waltz was announced - rather, bellowed - and the boys drifted away from me. It was evident that they did not intend to become wall flowers. For myself, it occurred to me that, except my somewhat debatable acquaintance with Miss King, I did not know a woman in the room. I called up all my courage and fortitude, and started toward her. I was determined to ask her to dance, and I got some chilly comfort out of the reflection that she couldn't do any worse than refuse; still, that would be quite bad enough, and I will not say that I crossed that room, with three or four hundred eyes upon me, in any oh-be-joyful frame of mind. I rather suspect that my face resembled that plebeian and oft-mentioned vegetable, the beet. I was within ten feet of her, and I was thinking that she couldn't possibly hold that cool, unconscious look much longer, when a hand feminine was extended from the row of silent watchers and caught at my sleeve.

"Ellie Carleton, it's never you!" chirped a familiar voice.

I turned, a bit dazed with the unexpected interruption, and saw that it was Edith Loroman, whom I had last seen in the East the summer before, when I was gyrating through Newport and all those places, with Barney MacTague for chaperon, and whom I had known for long. Edith had chosen to be very friendly always, and I liked her - only, I suspected her of being a bit too worldly to suit me.

"And why isn't it I? I can't see that my identity is more surprising than yours," I retorted, pulling myself together. It did certainly give me a start to see her there, and looking so exactly as she had always looked. I couldn't think of anything more to say, so, as the music had started, I asked her if she had any dances saved for me. I couldn't decently leave her and carry out my original plan, you see.

She laughed at my ignorance, and told me that this was a "frontier" dance, and there were no programs.

"You just promise one or two dances ahead," she explained. "As many as you can remember. Beryl told me all about how they do here; Beryl King is my cousin, you know."

I didn't know, but I was content to take her word for it, and asked her for that dance and got it, and she chattered on about everything under the sun, and told all about how they happened to be in Montana, and how long they were going to stay, and that Mr. Weaver had brought his auto, and another fellow - I forget his name - had intended to bring his, but didn't, and that they were going to tour through to Helena, on their way home, and it would be such fun, and that if I didn't come over right away to call upon her, she would never forgive me.

"There's a drawback," I told her. "I'm not on your cousin's visiting-list; I've never even been introduced to her."

"That," said Miss Edith complacently, "is easily remedied. You know mama well enough, I should think. Aunt Lodema - funny name, isn't it? - is stopping here all summer, with Beryl. Beryl has the strangest tastes. She *will* spend every summer out here with her father, and if any of us poor mortals want a glimpse of her between seasons, we must come where she is. She's a dear, and you must know her, even if you do hold yourself superior to us women. She's almost as much a crank on athletics as you are; you ought to see her on the links, once! That's why I can't understand her running away off here every summer. And, by the way, Ellie, what are *you* doing here - a stranger?"

"I'm earning my bread by the sweat of my brow," I told her plainly. "I'm a cowboy - a would-be, I suppose I should say."

She looked up at me horrified. "Have you - lost - your millions?" she wanted to know. Edith Loroman was always a straightforward questioner, at any rate.

"The millions," I told her, laughing, "are all right, I believe. Dad has a cattle-ranch in this part of the world, and he sent me out here to reform me. He meant it as a punishment, but at present I'm getting rather the best of the deal, I think."

"And where's Barney?" she asked. "One reason I came near not recognizing you was because you hadn't your shadow along."

"Barney is luxuriating in idleness somewhere," I answered lightly. "One couldn't expect *him* to turn savage, just because I did. I can't imagine Barney working for his daily bread."

"I can," retorted Miss Edith, "every bit as easily as I can imagine you! And, if you'll pardon me, I don't believe a word of it, either."

On the whole, I could hardly blame her. As she had always known me, I must have appeared to her somewhat like Solomon's lilies. But I did not try to convince her; there were other things more important.

I went and made my bow to Mrs. Loroman, and answered sundry questions - more conventional, I may say, than were those of her daughter. Mrs. Loroman was one of the best type of society dames, and I will own that I was a bit surprised to find that she was Beryl King's aunt. In spite of that indefinable little air of breeding that I had felt in my two meetings with Miss King, I had thought of her as distinctly a daughter of the range-land.

"I'll introduce you to my cousin and aunt now, if you like," Edith offered generously, in an undertone - for the two were not ten feet from us, although Miss King had not yet seen fit to know that I was in the room. How a woman can act so deuced innocent, beats me.

Miss King lowered her chin as much as half an inch, and looked at me as if I were an exceeding commonplace, inanimate object that could not possibly interest her. Her aunt, Lodema King, was almost as bad, I think; I didn't notice particularly. But Miss King's I-do-not-know-you-sir air could not save her; I hadn't schemed like a villain for a week, and ridden twenty-five miles at a good fast clip after a stiff day's work, just to be presented and walk away. I asked her for the next waltz.

"The next waltz is promised to Mr. Weaver," she told me freezingly.

I asked for the next two-step.

"The next two-step is also promised - to Mr. Weaver."

I began to have unfriendly feelings toward Mr. Weaver. "Will you be good enough to inform what dance is *not* promised?" I almost finished "to Mr. Weaver," but I'm not quite a cad, I hope.

"Really, we haven't programs here to-night," she parried.

I played a reckless lead. "I wonder," I said, looking straight down into those eyes of hers, and hoping she couldn't suspect the prickles chasing over me at the very look of them - "I wonder if it's because you're *afraid* to dance with me?"

"Are you so - fearsome?" she retorted evenly, and I got back instantly:

"It would almost seem so."

I had the satisfaction of seeing her lip go in between her teeth. (I should like to say something about those teeth - only it would sound like the advertisement of a dentifrice, for I should be bound to mention pearls once or twice.)

"You are flattering yourself, Mr. Carleton; I am not at all afraid to dance with you," she said - and, oh, the tone of her!

"I shall expect you to prove that instantly," I retorted, still looking straight into her face.

A quadrille - the old-fashioned kind - was called, and she looked up at me and put out her hand. Only an idiot would wonder whether I took it.

"This isn't a fair test," I told her, after leading her out in position. "You won't be dancing with me a quarter of the time, you know. Only the closest observer may tell, after we once get going, whom you are dancing with."

"That," she retorted, with a gleam in her eyes I couldn't - being no lady's man - interpret - "that is a mere quibble, and would not hold in court."

"It's going to hold in *this* court," I answered boldly, and wished I had not so systematically wasted my opportunities in the past - that I had spent more time drinking tea and studying the "infernal feminine."

She gave me a quick, puzzling glance, and as we were commanded at that instant to salute our partners, she swept me a half-curtsy that made me grit my teeth, though I tried to make my own bow quite as elaborate and mocking. I couldn't make her out at all during that dance. Whenever we came together there was that little air of mockery in every move she made, and yet something in her eyes seemed to invite and to challenge. The first time we were privileged, by the old-fashioned "caller," to "swing our partners," milady would have given me her finger-tips - only I wouldn't have it that way. I held her as close as I dared, and - I don't know but I'm a fool - she didn't seem in any great rage over it. Lord, how I did wish I was wise to the ways of women!

The next waltz I couldn't have, because she was to dance it with Mr. Weaver. So I had the fun of sitting there watching them fly around the room, and getting a good-sized dislike of the fellow over it. I don't pretend to be one of those large-minded men who are always painfully unprejudiced. Weaver looked like a pretty good sort, and under other circumstances I should probably have liked him, but as it was I emphatically did not.

However, I got a waltz, after a heart-breaking delay, and it was worth waiting for. I had felt all along that we could hit it off pretty well together, and we did. We didn't say much - we just floated off into another world - or I did - and there was nothing I wanted to say that I dared say. I call that a good excuse for silence.

Afterward I asked her for another, and she looked at me curiously.

"You're a very hard man to convince, Mr. Carleton," she told me, with that same queer look in her eyes. I was beginning to get drunk - intoxicated, if you like the word better - on those same eyes; they always affected me, somehow, as if I'd never seen them before; always that same little tingle of surprise went over me when she lifted those heavy fringes of lashes. I'm not psychologist enough to explain this, and I'm strictly no good at introspection; it was that way with me, and that will have to do.

I told her she probably would never meet another who required so much convincing, and, after wrangling over the matter politely for a minute, got her to promise me another waltz, said promise to be redeemed after supper.

I tried to talk to "Aunt Lodema," but she would have none of me, and she seemed to think I had more than my share of effrontery to attempt such a thing. Mrs. Loroman was better, and I filled in fifteen minutes or so very pleasantly with her. After that I went over to Edith and got her to sit out a dance with me.

The first thing she asked me was about Frosty. Who was he? and why was he here? and how long had he been here? I told her all I knew about him, and then turned frank and asked her why she wanted to know.

"Mama hasn't recognized him - yet," she said confidentially, "but I was sure he was the same. He has shaved his mustache, and he's much browner and heavier, but he's Fred Miller - and why doesn't he come and speak to me?"

Out of much words, I gathered that she and Frosty were, to put it mildly, old friends. She didn't just say there was an engagement between them, but she hinted it; his father had "had trouble" - the vagueness of women! - and Edith's mama had turned Frosty down, to put it bluntly. Frosty had, ostensibly, gone to South Africa, and that was the last of him. Miss Edith seemed quite disturbed over seeing him there in Kenmore. I told her that if Frosty wanted to stay in the background, that was his privilege and my gain, and she smiled at me vaguely and said of course it didn't really matter.

At supper-time our crowd got the storekeeper intimidated sufficiently to open his store and sell us something to eat. The King faction had looked upon us blackly, though there were too many of us to make it safe meddling, and none of us were minded to break bread with them. Instead, we sat around on the counter and on boxes in the store, and ate crackers and sardines and things like that. I couldn't help remembering my last Fourth, and the banquet I had given on board the *Molly Stark* - my yacht, named after the lady known to history, whom dad claims for an ancestress - and I laughed out loud. The boys wanted to know the cause of my mirth, and so, with a sardine laid out decently between two crackers in one hand, and a blue "granite" cup of plebeian beer in the other, I told them all about that banquet, and some of the things we had to eat and drink - whereat they laughed, too. The contrast was certainly amusing. But, somehow, I wouldn't have changed, just then, if I could have done so. That, also, is something I'm not psychologist enough to explain.

That last waltz with Miss King was like to prove disastrous, for we swished uncomfortably close to her father, standing scowling at Frosty and some of the others of our crowd near the door. Luckily, he didn't see us, and at the far end Miss King stopped abruptly. Her cheeks were pink, and her eyes looked up at me - wistfully, I could almost say.

"I think, Mr. Carleton, we had better stop," she said hesitatingly. "I don't believe your enmity is so ungenerous as to wish to cause me unpleasantness. You surely are convinced now that I am not afraid of you, so the truce is over."

I did not pretend to misunderstand. "I'm going home at

once," I told her gently, "and I shall take my spectacular crowd along with me; but I'm not sorry I came, and I hope you are not."

She looked at me soberly, and then away. "There is one thing I should like to say," she said, in so low a tone I had to lean to catch the words. "Please don't try to ride through King's Highway again; father hates you quite enough as it is, and it is scarcely the part of a gentleman to needlessly provoke an old man."

I could feel myself grow red. What a cad I must seem to her! "King's Highway shall be safe from my vandal feet hereafter," I told her, and meant it.

"So long as you keep that promise," she said, smiling a bit, "I shall try to remember mine enemy with respect."

"And I hope that mine enemy shall sometimes view the beauties of White Divide from a little distance - say half a mile or so," I answered daringly.

She heard me, but at that minute that Weaver chap came up, and she began talking to him as though he was her long-lost friend. I was clearly out of it, so I told Edith and her mother good night, bowed to "Aunt Lodema" and got the stony stare for my reward, and rounded up my crowd.

We passed old King in a body, and he growled something I could not hear; one of the boys told me, afterward, that it was just as well I didn't. We rode away under the stars, and I wished that night had been four times as long, and that Beryl King would be as nice to me as was Edith Loroman.

CHAPTER VII.

ONE DAY TOO LATE!

I suppose there is always a time when a fellow passes quite suddenly out of the cub-stage and feels himself a man - or, at least, a very great desire to be one. Until that Fourth of July life had been to me a playground, with an interruption or two to the game. When dad took such heroic measures to instil some sense into my head, he interrupted the game for ten days or so - and then I went back to my play, satisfied with new toys. At least, that is the way it seemed to me. But after that night, things were somehow different. I wanted to amount to something; I was absolutely ashamed of my general uselessness, and I came near writing to dad and telling him so.

The worst of it was that I didn't know just what it was I wanted to do, except ride over to that little pinnacle just out from King's Highway, and watch for Beryl King; that, of course, was out of the question, and maudlin, anyway.

On the third day after, as Frosty and I were riding circle quite silently and moodily together, we rode up into a little coulee on the southwestern side of White Divide, and came quite unexpectedly upon a little picnic-party camped comfortably down by the spring where we had meant to slake our own thirst. Of course, it was the Kings' house-party; they were the only luxuriously idle crowd in the country.

Edith and her mother greeted me with much apparent joy,

B. M. BOWER

but, really, I felt sorry for Frosty; all that saved him from recognition then was the providential near-sightedness of Mrs. Loroman. I observed that he was careful not to come close enough to the lady to run any risk.

Aunt Lodema tilted her chin at me, and Beryl - to tell the truth, I couldn't make up my mind about Beryl. When I first rode up to them, and she looked at me, I fancied there was a welcome in her eyes; after that there was anything else you like to name. I looked several times at her to make sure, but I couldn't tell any more what she was thinking than one can read the face of a Chinaman. (That isn't a pretty comparison, I know, but it gives my meaning, for, of all humans, Chinks are about the hardest to understand or read.) I was willing, however, to spend a good deal of time studying the subject of her thoughts, and got off my horse almost as soon as Mrs. Loroman and Edith invited me to stop and eat lunch with them. That Weaver fellow was not present, but another man, whom they introduced as Mr. Tenbrooke, was sitting dolefully on a rock, watching a maid unpacking eatables. Edith told me that "Uncle Homer" - which was old man King - and Mr. Weaver would be along presently. They had driven over to Kenmore first, on a matter of business.

Frosty, I could see, was not going to stay, even though Edith, in a polite little voice that made me wonder at her, invited him to do so. Edith was not the hostess, and had really no right to do that.

I tried to get a word with Miss Beryl, found myself having a good many words with Edith, instead, and in fifteen minutes I became as thoroughly disgusted with unkind fate as ever I've been in my life, and suddenly remembered that duty made further delay absolutely impossible. We rode away, with Edith protesting prettily at what she was pleased to call my bad manners.

For the rest of the way up that coulee Frosty and I were even more silent and moody than we had been before. The only time we spoke was when Frosty asked me gruffly how long those people expected to stay out here. I told him a week, and he grunted something under his breath about female fortune-hunters. I couldn't see what he was driving at, for I certainly should never think of accusing Edith and her mother of being that especial brand of abhorrence, but he was in a bitter mood, and I wouldn't argue with him then - I had troubles of my own to think of. I was beginning to call myself several kinds of a fool for letting a girl - however wonderful her eyes - give me bad half-hours quite so frequently; the thing had never happened to me before, and I had known hundreds of nice girls - approximately. When a fellow goes through a co-ed course, and has a dad whom the papers call financier, he gets a speaking-acquaintance with a few girls. The trouble with me was, I never gave the whole bunch as much thought as I was giving to Beryl King - and the more I thought about her, the less satisfaction there was in the thinking.

I waited a day or two, and then practically ran away from my work and rode over to that little butte. Some one was sitting on the same flat rock, and I climbed up to the place with more haste than grace, I imagine. When I reached the top, panting like the purr of the *Yellow Peril* - my automobile - when it gets warmed up and going smoothly, I discovered that it was Edith Loroman sitting placidly, with a camera on her knees, doing things to the internal organs of the thing. I don't know much about cameras, so I can't be more explicit.

"If it isn't Ellie, looking for all the world like the *Virginian* just stepped down from behind the footlights!" was her greeting. "Where in the world have you been, that you haven't been over to see us?"

"You must know that the palace of the King is closed against the Carletons," I, said, and I'm afraid I said it a bit crossly; I hadn't climbed that unmerciful butte just to bandy common-places with Edith Loroman, even if we were old friends. There are times when new enemies are more diverting than the oldest of old friends.

"Well, you could come when Uncle Homer is away - which he often is," she pouted. "Every Sunday he drives over to Kenmore and pokes around his miners and mines, and often Terence and Beryl go with him, so you could come -"

"No, thank you." I put on the dignity three deep there. "If I can't come when your uncle is at home, I won't sneak in when he's gone. I - how does it happen you are away out here by yourself?"

"Well," she explained, still doing things to the camera, "Beryl came out here yesterday, and made a sketch of the divide; I just happened to see her putting it away. So I made her tell me where she got that view-point, and I wanted her to come with me, so I could get a snap shot; it *is* pretty, from here. But she went over to the mines with Mr. Weaver, and I had to come alone. Beryl likes to be around those dirty mines - but I can't bear it. And, now I'm here, something's gone wrong with the thing, so I can't wind the film. Do you know how to fix it, Ellie?"

I didn't, and I told her so, in a word. Edith pouted again - she has a pretty mouth that looks well all tied up in a knot, and I have a slight suspicion that she knows it - and said that a fellow who could take an automobile all to pieces and put it together again ought to be able to fix a kodak. That's the way some women reason, I believe - just as though cars and kodaks are twin brothers.

Our conversation, as I remember it now, was decidedly flat and dull. I kept thinking of Beryl being there the day before - and I never knew; of her being off somewhere to-day with that Weaver fellow - and I knew it and couldn't do a thing. I hardly know which was the more unpleasant to dwell upon, but I do know that it made me mighty poor company for Edith. I sat there on a near-by rock and lighted cigarettes, only to let them go out, and glowered at King's Highway, off across the flat, as if it were the mouth of the bottomless pit. I can't wonder that Edith called me a bear, and asked me repeatedly if I had toothache, or anything.

By and by she had her kodak in working order again, and took two or three pictures of the divide. Edith is very pretty, I believe, and looks her best in short walking-costume. I wondered why she had not ridden out to the butte; Beryl had, the time I met her there, I remembered. She had a deep-chested blue roan that looked as if he could run, and I had noticed that she wore the divided skirt, which is so popular among women who ride. I don't, as a rule, notice much what women have on - but Beryl King's feet are altogether too small for the least observant man to pass over. Edith's feet were well shod, but commonplace.

"I wish you'd let me have one of those pictures when they're done," I told her, as amiably as I could.

She pushed back a lock of hair. "I'll send you one, if you like, when I get home. What address do you claim, in this wilderness?"

I wrote it down for her and went my way, feeling a badly used young man, with a strong inclination to quarrel with fate. Edith had managed, during her well-meant efforts at entertaining me, to couple Mr. Weaver's name all too frequently with that of her cousin. I found it very depressing - a good many things, in fact, were depressing that day.

I went back to camp and stuck to work for the rest of that week - until some of the boys told me that they had seen the Kings' guests scooting across the prairie in the big touring-car of Weaver's, evidently headed for Helena.

After that I got restless again, and every mile the round-up moved south I took as a special grievance; it put that much greater distance between me and King's Highway - and I had got to that unhealthy stage where every mile wore on my nerves, and all I wanted was to moon around that little butte. I believe I should even have taken a morbid pleasure in watching the light in her window o' nights, if it had been at all practicable.

CHAPTER VIII.

A FIGHT AND A RACE FOR LIFE.

It was between the spring round-up and the fall, while the boys were employed in desultory fashion at the home ranch, breaking in new horses and the like, and while I was indefatigably wearing a trail straight across country to that little butte - and getting mighty little out of it save the exercise and much heart-burnings - that the message came.

A man rode up to the corrals on a lather-gray horse, coming from Kenmore, where was a telephone-station connected from Osage. I read the message incredulously. Dad sick unto death? Such a thing had never happened - *couldn't* happen, it seemed to me. It was unbelievable; not to be thought of or tolerated. But all the while I was planning and scheming to shave off every superfluous minute, and get to where he was.

I held out the paper to Perry Potter, "Have some one saddle up Shylock," I ordered, quite as if he had been Rankin. "And Frosty will have to go with me as far as Osage. We can make it by to-morrow noon - through King's Highway. I mean to get that early afternoon train."

The last sentence I sent back over my shoulder, on my way to the house. Dad sick - dying? I cursed the miles between us. Frisco was a long, a terribly long, way off; it seemed in another world.

　　　　　B. M. BOWER

By then I was on my way back to the corral, with a decent suit of clothes on and a few things stuffed into a bag, and with a roll of money - money that I had earned - in my pocket. I couldn't have been ten minutes, but it seemed more. And Frisco was a long way off!

"You'd better take the rest of the boys part way," Potter greeted dryly as I came up.

I brushed past him and swung up into the saddle, feeling that if I stopped to answer I might be too late. I had a foolish notion that even a long breath would conspire to delay me. Frosty was already on his horse, and I noticed, without thinking about it at the time, that he was riding a long-legged sorrel, "Spikes," that could match Shylock on a long chase - as this was like to be.

We were off at a run, without once looking back or saying good-by to a man of them; for farewells take minutes in the saying, and minutes meant - more than I cared to think about just then. They were good fellows, those cowboys, but I left them standing awkwardly, as men do in the face of calamity they may not hinder, without a thought of whether I should ever see one of them again. With Frosty galloping at my right, elbow to elbow, we faced the dim, purple outline of White Divide.

Already the dusk was creeping over the prairie-land, and little sleepy birds started out of the grasses and flew protesting away from our rush past their nesting-places. Frosty spoke when we had passed out of the home-field, even in our haste stopping to close and tie fast the gate behind us.

"You don't want to run your horse down in the first ten miles, Ellis; we'll make time by taking it easy at first, and you'll get there just as soon." I knew he was right about it, and pulled Shylock down to the steady lope that was his natural gait. It was hard, though, to just "mosey" along as if we were starting out to kill time and earn our daily wage in the easiest possible manner. One's nerves demanded an unusual pace - a pace that would soothe fear by its very headlong race against misfortune.

Once or twice it occurred to me to wonder, just for a minute, how we should fare in King's Highway; but mostly my thoughts stuck to dad, and how it happened that he was "critically ill," as the message had put it. Crawford had sent that message; I knew from the precise way it was worded - Crawford never said *sick* - and Crawford was about as conservative a man as one could well be, and be human. He was as unemotional as a properly trained footman; Jenks, our butler, showed more feeling. But Crawford, if he was conservative, was also conscientious. Dad had had him for ten years, and trusted him a million miles farther than he would trust anybody else - for Crawford could no more lie than could the multiplication-table; if he said dad was "critically ill," that settled it; dad was. I used to tell Barney MacTague, when he thought it queer that I knew so little about dad's affairs, that dad was a fireproof safe, and Crawford was the combination lock. But perhaps it was the other way around; at any rate, they understood each other perfectly, and no other living man understood either.

The darkness flowed down over the land and hid the farther hills; the sky-line crept closer until White Divide seemed the boundary of the world, and all beyond its tumbled shade was untried mystery. Frosty, a shadowy figure rising and falling regularly beside me, turned his face and spoke again:

"We ought to make Pochette's Crossing by daylight, or a little after - with luck," he said. "We'll have to get horses from him to go on with; these will be all in, when we get that far."

"We'll try and sneak through the pass," I answered, putting unpleasant thoughts resolutely behind me. "We can't take time to argue the point out with old King."

"Sneak nothing," Frosty retorted grimly. "You don't know King, if you're counting on that."

I came near asking how he expected to get through, then; when I remembered my own spectacular flight, on a certain occasion, I felt that Frosty was calmly disowning our only hope.

We rode quietly into the mouth of King's Highway, our horses stepping softly in the deep sand of the trail as if they, too, realized the exigencies of the situation. We crossed the little stream that is the first baby beginning of Honey Creek - which flows through our ranch - with scarce a splash to betray our passing, and stopped before the closed gate. Frosty got down to swing it open, and his fingers touched a padlock doing business with bulldog pertinacity. Clearly, King was minded to protect himself from unwelcome evening callers.

"We'll have to take down the wires," Frosty murmured, coming back to where I waited. "Got your gun handy? Yuh might need it before long." Frosty was not warlike by nature, and when he advised having a gun handy I knew the situation to be critical.

We took down a panel of fence without interruption or sign of life at the house, not more than fifty yards away; Frosty whispered that they were probably at supper, and that it was our best time. I was foolish enough to regret going by without chance of a word with Beryl, great as was my haste. I had not seen her since that day Frosty and I had ridden into their picnic - though I made efforts enough, the Lord knows - and I was not at all happy over my many failures.

Whether it was good luck or bad, I saw her rise up from a hammock on the porch as we went by - for, as I said before, King's house was much closer to the trail than was decent; I could have leaned from the saddle and touched her with my quirt.

"Mr. Carleton" - I was fool enough to gloat over her instant recognition, in the dark like that - "what are you doing here - at this hour? Don't you know the risk? And your promise -"

She spoke in an undertone, as if she were afraid of being overheard - which I don't doubt she was.

But if she had been a Delilah she couldn't have betrayed me more completely. Frosty motioned imperatively for me to go on, but I had pulled up at her first word, and there I stood, waiting for her to finish, that I might explain that I had not lightly broken my promise; that I was compelled to cut off that extra sixty miles which would have made me, perhaps, too late. But I didn't tell her anything; there wasn't time. Frosty, waiting disapprovingly a length ahead, looked back and beckoned again insistently. At the same instant a door behind the girl opened with a jerk, and King himself bulked large and angry in the lamplight. Beryl shrank backward with a little cry - and I knew she had not meant to do me a hurt.

"Come on, you fool!" cried Frosty, and struck his horse savagely. I jabbed in my spurs, and Shylock leaped his length and fled down that familiar trail to the "gantlet," as I had always called it mentally after that second passing. But King, behind us, fired three shots quickly, one after another - and, as the bullets sang past, I knew them for a signal.

A dozen men, as it seemed to me, swarmed out from divers places to dispute our passing, and shots were being fired in the dark, their starting-point betrayed by vicious little spurts of flame. Shylock winced cruelly, as we whipped around the first shed, and I called out sharply to Frosty, still a length ahead. He turned just as my horse went down to his knees.

I jerked my feet from the stirrups and landed free and upright, which was a blessing. And it was then that I swung morally far back to the primitive, and wanted to kill, and kill, with never a thought for parley or retreat. Frosty, like the stanch old pal he was, pulled up and came back to me, though the bullets were flying fast and thick - and not wide enough for derision on our part.

"Jump up behind," he commanded, shooting as he spoke.

"We'll get out of this damned trap."

I had my doubts, and fired away without paying him much attention. I wanted, more than anything, to get the man who had shot down Shylock. That isn't a pretty confession, but it has the virtue of being the truth. So, while Frosty fired at the spurts of red and cursed me for stopping there, I crouched behind my dead horse and fought back with evil in my heart and a mighty poor aim.

Then, just as the first excitement was hardening into deliberate malevolence, came a clatter from beyond the house, and a chorus of familiar yells and the spiteful snapping of pistols. It was our boys - thirty of the biggest-hearted, bravest fellows that ever wore spurs, and, as they came thundering down to us, I could make out the bent, wiry figure of old Perry Potter in the lead, yelling and shooting wickeder than any one else in the crowd.

"Ellis!" he shouted, and I lifted up my voice and let him know that, like Webster, "I still lived." They came on with a rush that the King faction could not stay, to where I was ambushed between the solid walls of two sheds, with Shylock's bulk before me and Frosty swearing at my back.

"Horse hit?" snapped Perry Potter breathlessly. "I knowed it. Just like yuh. Get onto this'n uh mine - he's the best in the bunch - and light out - if yuh still want t' catch that train."

I came back from the primitive with a rush. I no longer wanted to kill and kill. Dad was lying "critically ill" in Frisco - and Frisco was a long way off! The miles between bulked big and black before me, so that I shivered and forgot my quarrel with King. I must catch that train.

I went with one leap up into the saddle as Perry Potter slid down, thought vaguely that I never could ride with the stirrups so short, but that there was not time to lengthen them; took my feet peevishly out of them altogether, and dashed down, that winding way between King's sheds and corrals while the Ragged H boys kept King's men at bay, and the unmusical medley of shots and yells followed us far in the darkness of the pass. At the last fence, where we perforce drew rein to make a free passage for our horses, I looked back, like one Mrs. Lot. A red glare lit the whole sky behind us with starry sparks, shooting up higher into the low-hanging crimson smoke-clouds. I stared, uncomprehending for a moment; then the thought of her stabbed through my brain, and I felt a sudden horror. "And Beryl's back among those devils!" I cried aloud, as I pulled my horse around.

"*Beryl*" - Frosty laid peculiar stress upon the name I had let slip - "isn't likely to be down among the sheds, where that fire is. Our boys are collecting damages for Shylock, I guess; hope they make a good job of it."

I felt silly enough just then to quarrel with my grandmother; I hate giving a man cause for thinking me a love-sick lobster, as I'd no doubt Frosty thought me. I led my horse over the wires he had let down, and we went on without stopping to put them back on the posts. It was some time before I spoke again, and, when I did, the subject was quite different; I was mourning because I hadn't the *Yellow Peril* to eat up the miles with.

"What good would that do yuh?" Frosty asked, with a composure I could only call unfeeling. "Yuh couldn't get a train, anyway, before the one yuh *will* get; motors are all right, in their place - but a horse isn't to be despised, either. I'd rather be stranded with a tired horse than a broken-down motor."

I did not agree with him, partly because I was not at all pleased with my present mount, and partly because I was not in amiable mood; so we galloped along in sulky silence, while a washed-out moon sidled over our heads and dodged behind cloud-banks quite as if she were ashamed to be seen. The coyotes got to yapping out somewhere in the dark, and, as we came among the breaks that border the Missouri, a gray wolf howled close at hand.

Perry Potter's horse, that had shown unmistakable symptoms of disgust at the endless gallop he had been called upon to maintain, shied sharply away from the sound, stumbled from leg-weariness, and fell heavily; for the second time that night I had need to show my dexterity - but, in this case, with Perry Potter's stirrups swinging somewhere in the vicinity of my knees, the danger of getting caught was not so great. I stood there in the dark loneliness of the silent hills and the howling wolf, and looked down at the brute with little pity and a good deal of resentment. I applied my toe tentatively to his ribs, and he just grunted. Frosty got down and led Spikes closer, and together we surveyed the heavily breathing, gray bulk in the sand at our feet.

"If he was the *Yellow Peril*, instead of one of your much-vaunted steeds," I remarked tartly, "I could go at him with a wrench and have him in working order again in five minutes; as it is -" I felt that the sentence was stronger uncompleted.

"As it is," finished Frosty calmly, "you'll just step up on Spikes and go on to Pochette's. It's only about ten miles, now; Spikes is good for it, if you ease him on the hills now and then. He isn't the *Yellow Peril*, maybe, but he's a good little horse, and he'll sure take yuh through the best he knows."

I don't know why, but a lump came up in my throat at the tone of him. I put out my hand and laid it on Spikes' wet, sweat-roughened neck. "Yes, he's a good little horse, and I beg his pardon for what I said," I owned, still with the ache just back of my palate. "But he can't carry us both, Frosty; I'll just have to tinker up this old skate, and make him go on."

"Yuh can't do it; he's reached his limit. Yuh can't expect a common cayuse like him to do more than eighty miles in one shift - at the gait we've been traveling. I'm surprised he's held out so long. Yuh take Spikes and go on; I'll walk in. Yuh know the way from here, and I can't help yuh out any more than to let yuh have Spikes. Go on - it's breaking day, and yuh haven't got any too much time to waste."

I looked at him, at Spikes standing wearily on three legs but with his ears perked gamily ahead, and down at the gray, worn-out horse of Perry Potter's. They have done what they could - and not one seemed to regret the service. I felt, at that moment, mighty small and unworthy, and tempted to reject the offer of the last ounce of endurance from either - for which I was not as deserving as I should have liked to be.

"You worked all day, and you've ridden all night, and gone without a mouthful of supper for me," I protested hotly. "And now you want to walk ten beastly miles of sand and hills. I won't -"

"Your dad cared enough to send for you -" he began, but I would not let him finish.

"You're right, Frosty," and I wrung his hand. "You're the real thing, and I'd do as much for you, old pal. I'll make that Frenchman rub Spikes down for an hour, or I'll kill him when I get back."

"You won't come back," said Frosty bruskly. "See that streak uh yellow, over there? Get a move on, if yuh don't want to miss that train - but ease Spikes up the hills!"

I nodded, pulled my hat down low over my eyes, and rode away; when I did get courage to glance back, Frosty still stood where I had left him, looking down at the gray horse.

An hour after sunrise I slipped off Spikes and watched them lead him away to the stable; he staggered like a man when he has drunk too long and deeply. I swallowed a cup of coffee, mounted a little buckskin, and went on, with Pochette's assurance, "Don't be afraid to put heem through," ringing in my ears. I was not afraid to put him through. That last forty-eight miles I rode mercilessly - for the demon of hurry was again urging me on. At ten o'clock I rolled stiffly off the buckskin at the Osage station, walked more stiffly into the office, and asked for a message. The operator handed me two, and looked at me with much curiosity - but I suppose I was a sight. The first was to tell me that a special would be ready at ten-thirty, and that the road would be cleared for it. I had not thought about a special - Osage being so far from Frisco; but Crawford was a wonder, and he had a long arm. My respect for Crawford increased amazingly as I read that message, and I began at once to bully the agent because the special was not ready at that minute to start. The second message was a laconic statement that dad was still alive; I folded it hurriedly and put it out of sight, for somehow it seemed to say a good many nasty things between the words.

I wired Crawford that I was ready to start and waiting for the special, and then I fumed and continued my bullying of the man in the office; he was not to blame for anything, of course, but it was a tremendous relief to take it out of somebody just then.

The special came, on time to a second, and I swung on and told the conductor to put her through for all she was worth - but he had already got his instructions as to speed, I fancy; we ripped down the track a mile a minute - and it wasn't long till we bettered that more than I'd have believed possible. The superintendent's car had been given over to me, I learned from the porter, and would carry me to Ogden, where dad's own car, the *Shasta*, would meet me. There, too, I saw the hand of Crawford; it was not like dad or him to borrow anything unless the necessity was absolute.

I hope I may never be compelled to take another such journey. Not that I was nervous at the killing pace we went - and it was certainly hair-raising, in places; but every curve that we whipped around on two wheels - approximately - told me that dad was in desperate case indeed, and that Crawford was oiling every joint with gold to get me there in time. At every division the crack engine of the shops was coupled on in seconds, rather than minutes, bellowed its challenge to all previous records, and scuttled away to the west; a new conductor swung up the steps and answered patiently the questions I hurled at him, and courteously passed over the invectives when I felt that we were crawling at a snail's pace and wanted him to hurry a bit.

At Ogden I hustled into the *Shasta* and felt a grain of comfort in its familiar atmosphere, and a sense of companionship in the solemn face of Cromwell Jones, our porter. I had taken many a jaunt in the old car, with Crom, and Rankin, and Tony, the best cook that ever fed a hungry man, and it seemed like coming home just to throw myself into my pet chair again, with Crom to fetch me something cold and fizzy.

From him I learned that it was pneumonia, and that if I got there in time it would be considered a miracle of speed and a triumph of faultless railroad system. If I had been tempted to take my ease and to sleep a bit, that settled it for me. The *Shasta* had no more power to lull my fears or to minister to my comfort. I refused to be satisfied with less than a couple of hundred miles an hour, and I was sore at the whole outfit because they refused to accommodate me.

Still, we got over the ground at such a clip that on the third day, with screech of whistle and clang of bell, we slowed at Oakland pier, where a crowd was cheering like the end of a race - which it was - and kodak fiends were underfoot as if I'd been somebody.

A motor-boat was waiting, and the race went on across the bay, where Crawford met me with the *Yellow Peril* at the ferry depot. I was told that I was in time, and when I got my hand on the wheel, and turned the *Peril* loose, it seemed, for the first time since leaving home, that fate was standing back and letting me run things.

Policemen waved their arms and said things at the way we went up Market Street, but I only turned it on a bit more and tried not to run over any humans; a dog got it, though, just as

B. M. BOWER

we whipped into Sacramento Street. I remember wishing that Frosty was with me, to be convinced that motors aren't so bad after all.

It was good to come tearing up the hill with the horn bellowing for a clear track, and to slow down just enough to make the turn between our bronze mastiffs, and skid up the drive, stopping at just the right instant to avoid going clear through the stable and trespassing upon our neighbor's flower-beds. It was good - but I don't believe Crawford appreciated the fact; imperturbable as he was, I fancied that he looked relieved when his feet touched the gravel. I was human enough to enjoy scaring Crawford a bit, and even regretted that I had not shaved closer to a collision.

Then I was up-stairs, in an atmosphere of drugs and trained nurses and funeral quiet, and knew for a certainty that I was still in time, and that dad knew me and was glad to have me there. I had never seen dad in bed before, and all my life he had been associated in my mind with calm self-possession and power and perfect grooming. To see him lying there like that, so white and weak and so utterly helpless, gave me a shock that I was quite unprepared for. I came mighty near acting like a woman with hysterics - and, coming as it did right after that run in the *Peril*, I gave Crawford something of a shock, too, I think. I know he got me by the shoulders and hustled me out of the room, and he was looking pretty shaky himself; and if his eyes weren't watery, then I saw exceedingly, crooked.

A doctor came and made me swallow something, and told me that there was a chance for dad, after all, though they had not thought so at first. Then he sent me off to bed, and Rankin appeared from somewhere, with his abominably righteous air, and I just escaped making another fool scene. But Rankin had the sense to take me in hand just as he used to do when I'd been having no end of a time with the boys, and so got me to bed. The stuff the doctor made me swallow did the rest, and I was dead to the world in ten minutes.

CHAPTER IX.

THE OLD LIFE - AND THE NEW.

Now that I was there, I was no good to anybody. The nurse wouldn't let me put my nose inside dad's door for a week, and I hadn't the heart to go out much while he was so sick. Rankin was about all the recreation I had, and he palled after the first day or two. I told him things about Montana that made him look painful because he hardly liked to call me a liar to my face; and the funny part was that I was telling him the truth.

Then dad got well enough so the nurse had no excuse for keeping me out, and I spent a lot of time sitting beside his bed and answering questions. By the time he was sitting up, peevish at the restraint of weakness and doctor's orders, we began to get really acquainted and to be able to talk together without a burdensome realization that we were father and son - and a mighty poor excuse for the son. Dad wasn't such bad company, I discovered. Before, he had been mostly the man that handled the carving-knife when I dined at home, and that wrote checks and dictated letters to Crawford in the privacy of his own den - he called it his study.

Now I found that he could tell a story that had some point to it, and could laugh at yours, in his dry way, whether it had any point or not. I even got to telling him some of the scrapes I had got into, and about Perry Potter; dad liked to hear about Perry Potter. The beauty of it was, he could understand everything; he had lived there himself long enough to get the

B. M. BOWER

range view-point. I hate telling a yarn and then going back over it explaining all the fine points.

I remember one night when the fog was rolling in from the ocean till you could hardly see the street-lamps across the way, we sat by the fire - dad was always great for big, wood fires - and smoked; and somehow I got strung out and told him about that Kenmore dance, and how the boys rigged up in my clothes and went. Dad laughed harder than I'd ever heard him before; you see, he knew the range, and the picture rose up before him all complete. I told that same yarn afterward to Barney MacTague, and there was nothing to it, so far as he was concerned. He said: "Lord! they must have been an out-at-heels lot not to have any clothes of their own." Now, what do you think of that?

Well, I went on from that and told dad about my flying trips through King's Highway, too - with the girl left out. Dad matched his finger-tips together while I was telling it, and afterward he didn't say much; only: "I knew you'd play the fool somehow, if you stayed long enough." He didn't explain, however, just what particular brand of fool I had been, or what he thought of old King, though I hinted pretty strong. Dad has got a smooth way of parrying anything he doesn't want to answer straight out, and it takes a fellow with more nerve than I've got to corner him and just make him give up an opinion if he doesn't want to. So I didn't find out a thing about that old row, or how it started - more than what I'd learned at the Ragged H, that is.

Frosty had written me, a week or two after I left, that our fellows had really burned King's sheds, and that Perry Potter had a bullet just scrape the hair off the top of his head, where he hadn't any to spare. It made him so mad, Frosty said, that he wanted to go back and kill, slay, and slaughter - that is Frosty's way of putting it. Another one of the boys had been hit in the arm, but it was only a flesh wound and nothing serious. So far as they could find out, King's men had got off without a scratch, Frosty said; which was another great sorrow to Perry Potter, who went around saying pointed things about poor markmanship and fellows who couldn't hit a barn if they were locked inside - that kept the boys stirred up and undecided whether to feel insulted or to take it as a joke. I wished that I was back there - until I read, down at the bottom of the last page, that Beryl King and her Aunt Lodema had gone back to the East.

The next day I learned the same thing from another source. Edith Loroman had kept her promise - as I remembered her, she wasn't great at that sort of thing, either - and sent me a picture of White Divide just before I left the ranch. Somehow, after that, we drifted into letter-writing. I wrote to thank her for the picture, and she wrote back to say "don't mention it" - in effect, at least, though it took three full pages to get that effect - and asked some questions about the ranch, and the boys, and Frosty Miller. I had to answer that letter and the questions - and that's how it began. It was a good deal of a nuisance, for I never did take much to pen work, and my conscience was hurting me half the time over delayed answers; Edith was always prompt; she liked to write letters better than I did, evidently.

But when she wrote, the day after I got that letter from Frosty, and said that Beryl and Aunt Lodema had just returned and were going to spend the winter in New York and join the Giddy Whirl, I will own that I was a much better - that is, prompt - correspondent. Edith is that kind of girl who can't write two pages without mentioning every one in her set; like those Local Items from little country towns; a paragraph for everybody.

So, having a strange and unwholesome hankering to hear all I could about Beryl, I encouraged Edith to write long and often by setting her an example. I didn't consider that I was taking a mean advantage of her, either, for she's the kind of girl who boasts about the number of her proposals and correspondents. I knew she'd cut a notch for me on the stick where she counted her victims, but it was worth the price, and I'm positive Edith didn't mind.

The only drawback was the disgusting frequency with which the words "Beryl and Terence Weaver" appeared; that did rather get on my nerves, and I did ask Edith once if Terence Weaver was the only man in New York. In fact, I was at one time on the point of going to New York myself and taking it out of Mr. Terence Weaver. I just ached to give him a run for his money. But when I hinted it - going to New York, I mean - dad looked rather hurt.

"I had expected you'd stay at home until after the holidays, at least," he remarked. "I'm old-fashioned enough to feel that a family should be together Christmas week, if at no other time. It doesn't necessarily follow that because there are only two left -" Dad dropped his glasses just then, and didn't finish the sentence. He didn't need to. I'd have stayed, then, no matter what string was pulling me to New York. It's so seldom, you see, that dad lowers his guard and lets you glimpse the real feeling there is in him. I felt such a cur for even wanting to leave him, that I stayed in that evening instead of going down to the Olympic, where was to be a sort of impromptu boxing-match between a couple of our swiftest amateurs.

Talking to dad was virtuous, but unexciting. I remember we discussed the profit, loss, and risk of cattle-raising in Montana, till bedtime came for dad. Then I went up and roasted Rankin for looking so damned astonished at my wanting to go to bed at ten-thirty. Rankin is unbearably righteous-looking, at times. I used often to wish he'd do something wicked, just to take that moral look off him; but the pedestal of his solemn virtue was too high for mere human temptations. So I had to content myself with shying a shoe his way and asking him what there was funny about me.

After dad got well enough to go back to watching his millions grow, and didn't seem to need me to keep him cheered up, life in our house dropped back to its old level - which means that I saw dad once a day, maybe. He gave me back my allowance and took to paying my bills again, and I was free to get into the old pace - which I will confess wasn't slow. The Montana incident seemed closed for good, and only Frosty's letters and a rather persistent memory was left of it.

In a month I had to acknowledge two emotions I hadn't counted on: surprise and disgust. I couldn't hit the old pace. Somehow, things were different - or I was different. At first I thought it was because Barney MacTague was away cruising around the Hawaii Islands, somewhere, with a party.

I came near having the *Molly Stark* put in commission and going after him; but dad wouldn't hear of that, and told me I'd better keep on dry land during the stormy months. So I gave in, for I hadn't the heart to go dead against his wishes, as I used to do. Besides, he'd have had to put up the coin, which he refused to do.

So I moped around the clubs, backed the light-weight champion of the hour for a big match, put up a pile of money on him, and saw it fade away and take with it my trust in champions. Dad was good about it, and put up what I'd gone over my allowance without a whimper. Then I chased around the country in the *Yellow Peril* and won three races down at Los Angeles, touring down and back with a fellow who had slathers of money, wore blue ties, and talked through his nose. I leave my enjoyment of the trip to your imagination.

When I got back, I had the *Yellow Peril* refitted and the tonneau put back on, and went in for society. I think that spell lasted as long as three weeks; I quit immensely popular with a certain bunch of widows and the like, and with a system so permeated with tea and bridge that it took a stiff course of high-balls and poker to take the taste out of my mouth.

I think it was in March that Barney came back; but he came back an engaged young man, so that in less than a week Barney began to pall. His fiancee had got him to swear off on poker and prize-fighting and smokers and everything. And I leave it

B. M. BOWER

to you if there would be much left of a fellow like Barney. All he was free to do - or wanted to do - was sit in a retired corner of the club with *Shasta* water and cigarettes for refreshments, and talk about Her, and how It had happened, and the pangs of uncertainty that shot through his heart till he knew for sure. Barney's full as tall as I am, and he weighs twenty-five pounds more; and to hear a great, hulking brute like that talking slush was enough to make a man forswear love in all forms forever. He'd show me her picture regular, every time I met him, and expect me to hand out a jolly. She wasn't so much, either. Her nose was crooked, and she didn't appear to have any eyebrows to speak of. I'd like to have him see - well, a certain young woman with eyelashes and - Oh, well, it wasn't Barney's fault that he'd never seen a real beauty, and so was satisfied with his particular Her. I began to shy at Barney, and avoided him as systematically as if I owed him money; which I didn't. I just couldn't stand for so much monologue with a girl with no eyebrows and a crooked nose for the never-failing subject.

My next unaccountable notion was manifested in an unreasoning dislike of Rankin. He got to going to some mission-meetings, somewhere down near the Barbary Coast; I got out of him that much, and that he sometimes led the meetings. Rankin can't lie - or won't - so he said right out that he was doing what little he could to save precious souls. That part was all right, of course; but he was so beastly solemn and sanctimonious that he came near sending my soul - maybe it isn't as precious as those he was laboring with - straight to the bad place.

Every morning when he appeared like the ghost of a Puritan ancestor's remorse at my bedside, I swore I'd send him off before night. To look at him you'd think I had done a murder and he was an eye-witness to the deed. Still, it's pretty raw to send a man off just because he's the embodiment of punctiliousness and looks virtuously grieved for your sins. In his general demeanor, I admit that Rankin was quite irreproachable - and that's why I hated him so.

Besides, Montana had spoiled me for wanting to be dressed like a baby, and I would much rather get my own hat and stick; I never had the chance, though. I'd turn and find him just back of my elbow, with the things in his hands and that damned righteous look on his face, and generally I'd swear he did get on my nerves so.

I'm afraid I ruined him for a good servant, and taught him habits of idleness he'll never outgrow; for every morning I'd send him below - I won't state the exact destination, but I have reasons for thinking he never got farther than the servants' hall - with strict - and for the most part profane - orders not to show his face again unless I rang. Even at that, I always found him waiting up for me when I came home. Oh, there was no changing the ways of Rankin.

I think it was about the middle of May when my general discontent with life in the old burgh took a virulent form. I'd been losing a lot one way and another, and Barney and I had come together literally and with much force when we were having a spurt with our cars out toward Ingleside. The Yellow Peril looked pretty sick when I picked myself out of the mess and found I wasn't hurt except in my feelings. Barney's car only had the lamps smashed, and as he had run into me, that made me sore. We said things, and I caught a street-car back to town. Barney drove in, about as hot as I was, I guess.

So, when I got home and found a letter from Frosty, my mind was open for something new. The letter was short, but it did the business and gave me a hunger for the old days that nothing but a hard gallop over the prairie-lands, with the wind blowing the breath out of my nostrils, could satisfy. He said the round-up would start in about a week. That was about all, but I got up and did something I'd never done before.

I took the letter and went straight down to dad's private den and interrupted him when he was going over his afternoon letters with Crawford. Dad was very particular not to be interrupted at such times; his mail-hours were held sacred, and

B. M. BOWER

nothing short of a life-or-death matter would have taken me in there - in any normal state of mind.

Crawford started out of his chair - if you knew Crawford that one action would tell you a whole lot - and dad whirled toward me and asked what had happened. I think they both expected to hear that the house was on fire.

"The round-up starts next week, dad," I blurted, and then stopped. It just occurred to me that it might not sound important to them.

Dad matched his finger-tips together. "Since I first bought a bunch of cattle," he drawled, "the round-up has never failed to start some time during this month. Is it vitally important that it should *not* start?"

"*I've* got to start at once, or I can't catch it." I fancied, just then, that I detected a glimmer of amusement on Crawford's face. I wanted to hit him with something.

"Is there any reason why it must be caught?" dad wanted to know, in his worst tone, which is almost diabolically calm.

"Yes," I rapped out, growing a bit riled, "there is. I can't stand this do-nothing existence any longer. You brought me up to it, and never let me know anything about your business, or how to help you run it -"

"It never occurred to me," drawled dad, "that I needed help to run my business."

"And last spring you rose up, all of a sudden, and started in to cure me of being a drone. The medicine you used was strong; it did the business pretty thoroughly. You've no kick coming at the result. I'm going to start to-morrow."

Dad looked at me till I began to feel squirmy. I've thought since that he wasn't as surprised as I imagined, and that, on the whole, he was pleased. But, if he was, he was mighty careful not to show it.

"You would better give me a list of your debts, then," he said laconically. "I shall see that your allowance goes on just the same; you may want to invest in - er - cattle."

"Thank you, dad," I said, and turned to go.

"And I wish to Heaven," he called after me, "that you'd take Rankin along and turn him loose out there. He might do to herd sheep. I'm sick of that hark-from-the-tombs face of his. I made a footman of him while you were gone before, rather than turn him off; but I'm damned if I do it again."

I stopped just short of the door and grinned back at him. "Rankin," I said, "is one of the horrors I'm trying to leave behind, dad."

But dad had gone back to his correspondence. "In regard to that Clark, Marsden, and Clark affair, I think, Crawford, it would be well -"

I closed the door quietly and left them. It was dad's way, and I laughed a little to myself as I was going back to my room to round up Rankin and set him to packing. I meant to stand over him with a club this time, if necessary, and see that I got what I wanted packed.

The next evening I started again for Montana - and I didn't go in dad's private car, either. Save for the fact that I had no grievance with him, and that we ate dinner alone together and drank a bottle of extra dry to the success of my pilgrimage, I went much as I had gone before: humbly and unheralded except for a telegram for some one to meet me at Osage.

Rankin, I may say, did not go with me, though I did as dad had suggested and offered to take him along and get him a job herding sheep. The memory of Rankin's pained countenance lingers with me yet, and cheers me in many a dark hour when there's nothing else to laugh over.

CHAPTER X.

I SHAKE HANDS WITH OLD MAN KING.

For the second time in my irresponsible career I stood on the station platform at Osage and watched the train slide off to the East. It's a blamed fool who never learns anything by experience, and I never have accused myself of being a fool - except at odd times - so I didn't land broke. I had money to pay for several meals, and I looked around for somebody I knew; Frosty, I hoped.

For the sodden land I had looked upon with such disgust when first I had seen it, the range lay dimpled in all the enticement of spring. Where first I had seen dirty snow-banks, the green was bright as our lawn at home. The hilltops were lighter in shade, and the jagged line of hills in the far distance was a soft, soft blue, just stopping short of reddish-purple. I'm not the sort of human that goes wading to his chin in lights and shades and dim perspectives, and names every tone he can think of - especially mauve; they do go it strong on mauve - before he's through. But I did lift my hat to that dimply green reach of prairie, and thanked God I was there.

I turned toward the hill that hid the town, and there came Frosty driving the same disreputable rig that had taken me first to the Bay State. I dropped my suit-case and gripped his hand almost before he had pulled up at the platform. Lord! but I was glad to see that thin, brown face of his.

"Looks like we'd got to be afflicted with your presence another summer," he grinned. "I hope yuh ain't going to claim I coaxed yuh back, because I took particular pains not to. And, uh course, the boys are just dreading the sight of yuh. Where's your war-bag, darn yuh?"

How was that for a greeting? It suited me, all right. I just thumped Frosty on the back and called him a name that it would make a lady faint to hear, and we laughed like a couple of fools.

I'm not on oath, perhaps, but still I feel somehow bound to tell all the truth, and not to pass myself off for a saint. So I will say that Frosty and I had a celebration, that night; an Osage, Montana, celebration, with all the fixings. Know the brand - because if you don't, I'd hang before I'd tell just how many shots we put through ceilings, or how we rent the atmosphere outside. You see, I was glad to get back, and Frosty was glad to have me back; and since neither of us are the fall-on-your-neck-and-put-a-ring-on-your-finger kind, we had to exuberate some other way; and, as Frosty, would put it, "We sure did."

I can't say we felt quite so exuberant next morning, but we were willing to take our medicine, and started for the ranch all serene. I won't say a word about mauves and faint ambers and umbras, but I do want to give that country a good word, as it looked that morning to me. It was great.

There are plenty of places can put it all over that Osage country for straight scenery, but I never saw such a contented-looking place as that big prairie-land was that morning. I've seen it with the tears running down its face, and pretty well draggled and seedy; but when we started out with the sun shining against our cheeks and the hills looking so warm and lazy and the hollows kind of smiling to themselves over something, and the prairie-dogs gossiping worse than a ladies' self-culture meeting, I tell you, it all looked good to me, and I told Frosty so.

"I'd rather be a forty-dollar puncher in this man's land," I enthused, "than a lily-of-the-field somewhere in civilization."

"In other words," Frosty retorted sarcastically, "you *think* you prefer the canned vegetables and contentment, as the Bible says, to corn-fed beefsteak and homesickness thereby. But you wait till yuh get to the ranch and old Perry Potter puts yuh through your paces. You'll thank the Lord every Sundown that yuh *ain't* a forty-dollar man that has got to drill right along or get fired; you'll pat yourself on the back more than once that you've got a cinch on your job and can lay off whenever yuh feel like it. From all the signs and tokens, us Ragged H punchers'll be wise to trade our beds off for lanterns to ride by. Your dad's bought a lot more cattle, and they've drifted like hell; we've got to cover mighty near the whole State uh Montana and part uh South Africa to gather them in."

"You're a blamed pessimist," I told him, "and you can't give me cold feet that easy. If you knew how I ache to get a good horse under me -"

"Thought they had horses out your way," Frosty cut in.

"A range-horse, you idiot, and a range-saddle. I did ride some on a fancy-gaited steed with a saddle that resembled a porus plaster and stirrups like a lady's bracelet; it didn't fill the aching void a little bit."

"Well, maybe yuh won't feel any aching void out here," he said, "but if yuh follow round-up this season you'll sure have plenty of other brands of ache."

I told him I'd be right with them at the finish, and he needn't to worry any about me. Pretty soon I'll show you how well I kept my word. We rode and rode, and handed out our experiences to each other, and got to Pochette's that night. I couldn't help remembering the last time I'd been over that trail, and how rocky I felt about things. Frosty said he wasn't worried about that walk of his into Pochette's growing dim in his memory, either.

Well, then, we got to Pochette's - I think I have remarked the fact. And at Pochette's, just unharnessing his team, limped my friend of White Divide, old King. Funny how a man's viewpoint will change when there's a girl cached somewhere in the background. Not even the memory of Shylock's stiffening limbs could bring me to a mood for war. On the contrary, I felt more like rushing up and asking him how were all the folks, and when did Beryl expect to come home. But not Frosty; he drove phlegmatically up so that there was just comfortable space for a man to squeeze between our rig and King's, hopped out, and began unhooking the traces as if there wasn't a soul but us around. King was looping up the lines of his team, and he glared at us across the backs of his horses as if we were - well, caterpillars at a picnic and he was a girl with nice clothes and a fellow and a set of nerves. His next logical move would be to let out a squawk and faint, I thought; in which case I should have started in to do the comforting, with a dipper of water from the pump. He didn't faint, though.

I walked around and let down the neck-yoke, and his eyes followed me with suspicion. "Hello, Mr. King," I sang out in a brazen attempt to hypnotize him into the belief we were friends. "How's the world using you, these days?"

"Huh!" grunted the unhypnotized one, deep in his chest.

Frosty straightened up and looked at me queerly; he said afterward that he couldn't make out whether I was trying to pull off a gun fight, or had gone dippy.

But I was only in the last throes of exuberance at being in the country at all, and I didn't give a damn what King thought; I'd made up my mind to be sociable, and that settled it.

"Range is looking fine," I remarked, snapping the inside checks back into the hame-rings. "Stock come through the winter in good shape?" Oh, I had my nerve right along with me.

"You go to hell," advised King, bringing out each word fresh-coined and shiny with feeling.

"I was headed that way," I smiled across at him, "but at the last minute I gave Montana first choice; I knew you were still here, you see."

He let go the bridle of the horse he was about to lead away to the stable, and limped around so that he stood within two feet of me. "Yuh want to -" he began, and then his mouth stayed open and silent.

I had reached out and got him by the hand, and gave him a grip - the grip that made all the fellows quit offering their paws to me in Frisco.

"Put it there, King!" I cried idiotically and as heartily as I knew how. "Glad to see you. Dad's well and busy as usual, and sends regards. How's your good health?"

He was squirming good and plenty, by that time, and I let him go. I acted the fool, all right, and I don't tell it to have any one think I was a smart young sprig; I'm just putting it out straight as it happened.

Frosty stood back, and I noticed, out of the tail of my eye, that he was ready for trouble and expecting it to come in bunches; and I didn't know, myself, but what I was due for new ventilators in my system.

But King never did a thing but stand and hold his hand and look at me. I couldn't even guess at what he thought. In half a minute or less he got his horse by the bridle again - with his left hand - and went limping off ahead of us to the stable, saying things in his collar.

"You blasted fool," Frosty muttered to me. "You've done it

B. M. BOWER

real pretty, this time. That old Siwash'll cut your throat, like as not, to pay for all those insulting remarks and that hand-shake."

"First time I ever insulted a man by shaking hands and telling him I was glad to see him," I retorted. "And I don't think it will be necessary for you to stand guard over my jugular to-night, either. That old boy will take a lot of time to study out the situation, if I'm any judge. You won't hear a peep out of him, and I'll bet money on it."

"All right," said Frosty, and his tone sounded dubious. "But you're the first Ragged H man that has ever walked up and shook hands with the old devil. Perry Potter himself wouldn't have the nerve."

Now, that was a compliment, but I don't believe I took it just the way Frosty meant I should. I was proud as thunder to have him call me a "Ragged H man" so unconsciously. It showed that he really thought of me simply as one of the boys; that the "son and heir" view-point - oh, that had always rankled, deep down where we bury unpleasant things in our memory - had been utterly forgotten. So the tribute to my nerve didn't go for anything beside that. I was a "Ragged H man," on the same footing as the rest of them. It's silly owning it, but it gave me a little tingle of pleasure to have one of dad's men call dad's son and heir "a blasted fool." I don't believe the Lord made me an aristocrat.

We didn't see anything more of King till supper was called. At Pochette's you sit down to a long table covered with dark-red mottled oilcloth and sprinkled with things to eat, and watch that your elbow doesn't cause your nearest neighbor to do the sword-swallowing act involuntarily and disastrously with his knife, or - you don't eat. Frosty and I had walked down to the ferry-crossing while we waited, and then were late getting into the game when we heard the summons.

We went in and sat down just as the Chinaman was handing

thick cups of coffee around rather sloppily. From force of habit I looked for my napkin, remembered that I was in a napkinless region, and glanced up to see if any one had noticed.

Just across from me old King was pushing back his chair and getting stiffly upon his feet. He met my eyes squarely - friend or enemy, I like a man to do that - and scowled.

"Through already?" I reached for the sugar-bowl.

"What's it to you, damn yuh?" he snapped, but we could see at a glance that King had not begun his meal.

I looked at Frosty, and he seemed waiting for me to say something. So I said: "Too bad - we Ragged H men are such mighty slow eaters. If it's on my account, sit right down and make yourself comfortable. I don't mind; I dare say I've eaten in worse company."

He went off growling, and I leaned back and stirred my coffee as leisurely as if I were killing time over a bit of crab in the Palace, waiting for my order to come. Frosty, I observed, had also slowed down perceptibly; and so we "toyed with the viands" just like a girl in a story - in real life, I've noticed, girls develop full-grown appetites and aren't ashamed of them. King went outside to wait, and I'm sure I hope he enjoyed it; I know we did. We drank three cups of coffee apiece, ate a platter of fried fish, and took plenty of time over the bones, got into an argument over who was Lazarus with the fellow at the end of the table, and were too engrossed to eat a mouthful while it lasted. We had the bad manners to pick our teeth thoroughly with the wooden toothpicks, and Frosty showed me how to balance a knife and fork on a toothpick - or, perhaps, it was two - on the edge of his cup. I tried it several times, but couldn't make it work.

The others had finished long ago and were sitting around next the wall watching us while they smoked. About that time King put his head in at the door, and looked at us.

B. M. BOWER

"Just a minute," I cheered him. Frosty began cracking his prune-pits and eating the meats, and I went at it, too. I don't like prune-pits a little bit.

The pits finished, Frosty looked anxiously around the table. There was nothing more except some butter that we hadn't the nerve to tackle single-handed, and some salt and a bottle of ketchup and the toothpicks. We went at the toothpicks again; until Frosty got a splinter stuck between his teeth, and had a deuce of a time getting it out.

"I've heard," he sighed, when the splinter lay in his palm, "that some state dinners last three or four hours; blamed if I see how they work it. I'm through. I lay down my hand right here - unless you're willing to tackle the ketchup. If you are, I stay with you, and I'll eat half." He sighed again when he promised.

For answer I pushed back my chair. Frosty smiled and followed me out. For the satisfaction of the righteous I will say that we both suffered from indigestion that night, which I suppose was just and right.

CHAPTER XI.

A CABLE SNAPS.

Our lazy land smiling and dreaming to itself had disappeared; in its stead, the wind howled down the river from the west and lashed the water into what would have looked respectable waves to one who had not been on the ocean and seen the real thing. The new grass lay flat upon the prairies, and chunks of dirt rattled down from the roof of Pochette's primitive abiding-place. It is true the sun shone, but I really wouldn't have been at all surprised if the wind had blown it out, 'most any time.

Pochette himself looked worried when we trooped in to breakfast. (By the way, old King never showed up till we were through; then he limped in and sat down to the table without a glance our way.) While we were smoking, over by the fireplace, Pochette came sidling up to us. He was a little skimpy man with crooked legs, a real French cut of beard, and an apologetic manner. I think he rather prided himself upon his familiarity with the English language - especially that part which is censored so severely by editors that only a half-dozen words are permitted to appear in cold type, and sometimes even they must hide their faces behind such flimsy veils as this: d - n. So if I never quote Mr. Pochette verbatim, you'll know why.

"I theenk you will not wish for cross on the reever, no?" he began ingratiatingly. "The weend she blow lak ------, and my

B. M. BOWER

boat, she zat small, she ----."

I caught King looking at us from under his eyebrows, so I was airily indifferent to wind or water. "Sure, we want to cross," I said. "Just as soon as we finish our smoke, Pochette."

"But, mon Dieu!" (Ever hear tell of a Frenchman that didn't begin his sentences that way? In this case, however, Pochette really said just that.) "The weend, she blow lak -"

"'A hurricane; bimeby by she blaw some more,'" I quoted bravely. "It's all right, Pochette; let her howl. We're going to cross, just the same. It isn't likely you'll have to make the trip for any body else to-day." I didn't mean to, but I looked over toward King, and caught the glint of his unfriendly eyes upon me. Also, the corners of his mouth hunched up for a second in what looked like a sneer. But the Lord knows I wasn't casting any aspersions on *his* nerve.

He must have taken it that way, though; for he went out when we did and hooked up, and when we drove down to where the little old scow they called a ferry was bobbing like a decoy-duck in the water, he was just behind us with his team. Pochette looked at him, and at us, and at the river; and his meager little face with its pointed beard looked like a perturbed gnome - if you ever saw one.

"The leetle boat, she not stand for ze beeg load. The weend, she -"

"Aw, what yuh running a ferry for?" Frosty cut in impatiently. "There's a good, strong current on, to-day; she'll go across on a high run."

Pochette shook his head still more dubiously, till I got down and bolstered up his courage with a small piece of gold. They're all alike; their courage ebbs and flows on a golden tide, if you'll let me indulge in a bit of unnecessary hyperbole. He worked the scow around end on to the bank, so that we could drive on. The team wasn't a bit stuck on going, but Frosty knows how to handle horses, and they steadied when he went to their heads and talked to them.

We were so busy with our own affairs that we didn't notice what was going on behind us till we heard Pochette declaiming bad profanity in a high soprano. Then I turned, and he was trying to stand off old King. But King wasn't that sort; he yelled to us to move up and make room, and then took down his whip and started up. Pochette pirouetted out of the way, and stood holding to the low plank railing while he went on saying things that, properly pronounced, must have been very blasphemous.

King paid about as much attention to him as he would to a good-sized prairie-dog chittering beside its burrow. I reckon he knew Pochette pretty well. He got his rig in place and climbed down and went to his horses' heads.

"Now, shove off, dammit," he ordered, just as if no one had been near bursting a blood-vessel within ten feet of him.

Pochette gulped, worked the point of his beard up and down like a villain in a second-rate melodrama, and shoved off. The current and the wind caught us in their grip, and we swashed out from shore and got under way.

I can't say that trip looked good to me, from the first rod out. Of course, the river couldn't rear up and get real savage, like the ocean, but there were choppy little waves that were plenty nasty enough, once you got to bucking them with a blum-nosed old scow fastened to a cable that swayed and sagged in the wind that came howling down on us. And with two rigs on, we filled her from bow to stern; all but about four feet around the edges.

Frosty looked across to the farther shore, then at the sagging cable, and then at me. I gathered that he had his doubts, too, but he wouldn't say anything. Nobody did, for that matter.

Even Pochette wasn't doing anything but chew his whiskers and watch the cable.

Then she broke, with a snap like a rifle, and a jolt that came near throwing us off our feet. Pochette gave a yell and relapsed into French that I'd hate to translate; it would shock even his own countrymen. The ferry ducked and bobbed, now there was nothing to hold its nose steady to the current, and went careering down river with all hands aboard and looking for trouble.

We didn't do anything, though; there wasn't anything to do but stay right where we were and take chances. If she stayed right side up we would probably land eventually. If she flopped over - which she seemed trying to do, we'd get a cold bath and lose our teams, if no worse.

Soon as I thought of that, I began unhooking the traces of the horse nearest. The poor brutes ought at least to have a chance to swim for it. Frosty caught on, and went to work, too, and in half a minute we had them free of the wagon and stripped of everything but their bridles. They would have as good a show as we, and maybe better.

I looked back to see what King was doing. He was having troubles of his own, trying to keep one of his cayuses on all its feet at once. It was scared, poor devil, and it took all his strength on the bit to keep it from rearing and maybe upsetting the whole bunch. Pochette wasn't doing anything but lament, so I went back and unhooked King's horses for him, and took off the harness and threw it in the back of his wagon so they wouldn't tangle their feet in it when it came to a show-down.

I don't think he was what you could call grateful; he never looked my way at all, but went on cussing the horse he was holding, for acting up just when he should keep his wits. I went back to Frosty, and we stood elbows touching, waiting for whatever was coming.

For what seemed a long while, nothing came but wind and water. But I don't mind saying that there was plenty of that, and if either one had been suddenly barred out of the game we wouldn't any of us have called the umpire harsh names. We drifted, slippety-slosh, and the wind ripped holes in the atmosphere and made our eyes water with the bare force of it when we faced the west. And none of us had anything to say, except Pochette; he said a lot, I remember, but never mind what. I don't suppose he was mentally responsible at the time.

Then, a long, narrow, yellow tongue of sand-bar seemed to reach right out into the river and lap us up. We landed with a worse jolt than when we broke away from the cable, and the gray-blue river went humping past without us. Frosty and I looked at each other and grinned; after all, we were coming out of the deal better than we had expected, for we were still right side up and on the side of the river toward home. We were a mile or so down river from the trail, but once we were on the bank with our rig, that was nothing.

We had landed head on, with the nose of the scow plowed high and dry. Being at the front, we went at getting our team off, and our wagon. There was a four or five-foot jump to make, and the horses didn't know how about it, at first. But with one of us pulling, and the other slashing them over the rump, they made it, one at a time. The sand was soft and acted something like quicksand, too, and we hustled them to shore and tied them to some bushes. The bank was steep there, and we didn't know how we were going to make the climb, but we left that to worry over afterward; we still had our rig to get ashore, and it began to look like quite a contract.

We went back, with our boot tracks going deep, and then filling up and settling back almost level six steps behind us. Frosty looked back at them and scowled.

"For sand that isn't quicksand," he said, "this layout will stand about as little monkeying with as any sand I ever met up with. Time we make a few trips over it, she's going to be pudding without the raisins. And that's a picnic, with our rig on the main deck, as you might say."

We went back and sat swinging our legs off the free board end of the ferry boat, and rolled us a smoke apiece and considered the next move. King was somewhere back between our rig and his, cussing Pochette to a fare-you-well for having such a rotten layout and making white men pay good money for the privilege of risking their lives and property upon it.

"We'll have to unload and take the wagon to pieces and pack everything ashore - I guess that's our only show," said Frosty. We had just given up my idea of working the scow up along the bar to the bank. We couldn't budge her off the sand, and Pochette warned us that if we did the wind would immediately commence doing things to us again.

Frosty's idea seemed the only possible way, so we threw away our cigarettes and got ready for business; the dismembering and carrying ashore of that road-wagon promised to be no light task. Frosty yelled to Pochette to come and get busy, and went to work on the rig. It looked to me like a case where we were all in the same fix, and personal spite shouldn't count for anything, but King was leaning against the wheel of his buggy, cramming tobacco into his stubby pipe - the same one apparently that I had rescued from the pickle barrel - and, seeing the wind scatter half of it broadcast, as though he didn't care a rap whether he got solid earth beneath his feet once more, or went floating down the river. I wanted to propose a truce for such time as it would take to get us all safe on terra firma, but on second thoughts I refrained. We could get off without his help, and he was the sort of man who would cheerfully have gone to his last long sleep at the bottom of that boiling river rather than accept the assistance of an enemy.

The next couple of hours was a season of aching back, and sloppy feet, and grunting, and swearing that I don't much care about remembering in detail. The wind blew till the tears ran down our cheeks. The sand stuck and clogged every move we made till I used to dream of it afterward. If you think it was just a simple little job, taking that rig to pieces and packing it to dry land on our backs, just give another guess. And if you think we were any of us in a mood to look at it as a joke, you're miles off the track.

Pochette helped us like a little man - he had to, or we'd have done him up right there. Old King sat on the ferry-rail and smoked, and watched us break our backs sardonically - I did think I had that last word in the wrong place; but I think not. We did break our backs sardonically, and he watched us in the same fashion; so the word stands as she is.

When the last load was safe on the bank, I went back to the boat. It seemed a low-down way to leave a man, and now he knew I wasn't fishing for help, I didn't mind speaking to the old reprobate. So I went up and faced him, still sitting on the ferry-rail, and still smoking.

"Mr. King," I said politely as I could, "we're all right now, and, if you like, we'll help you off. It won't take long if we all get to work."

He took two long puffs, and pressed the tobacco down in his pipe. "You go to hell," he advised me for the second time. "When I want any help from you or your tribe, I'll let yuh know."

It took me just one second to backslide from my politeness. "Go to the devil, then!" I snapped. "I hope you have to stay on the damn' bar a week." Then I went plucking back through the sand that almost pulled the shoes off my feet every step, kicking myself for many kinds of a fool. Lord, but I was mad!

Pochette went back to the boat and old King, after nearly getting kicked into the river for hinting that we ought to pay for the damage and trouble we had caused him. Frosty and I weren't in any frame of mind for such a hold-up, and it didn't take him long to find it out.

B. M. BOWER

The bank there was so steep that we had to pack my trunk and what other truck had been brought out from Osage, up to the top by hand. That was another temper-sweetening job. Then we put the wagon together, hitched on the horses, and they managed to get to the top with it, by a scratch. It all took time - and, as for patience, we'd been out of that commodity for so long we hardly knew it by name.

The last straw fell on us just as we were loading up. I happened to look down upon the ferry; and what do you suppose that old devil was doing? He had torn up the back part of the plank floor of the ferry, and had laid it along the sand for a bridge. He had made an incline from boat nose to the bar, and had rough-locked his wagon and driven it down. Just as we looked, he had come to the end of his bridge, and he and Pochette were taking up the planks behind and extending the platform out in front.

Well! maybe you think Frosty and I stood there congratulating the old fox. Frosty wanted me to kick him, I remember; and he said a lot of things that sounded inspired to me, they hit my feelings off so straight. If we had had the sense to do what old King was doing, we'd have been ten or fifteen miles nearer home than we were.

But, anyway, we were up the bank ahead of him, and we loaded in the last package and drove away from the painful scene at a lope. And you can imagine how we didn't love old King any better, after that experience.

CHAPTER XII.

I BEGIN TO REALIZE.

If I had hoped that I'd gotten over any foolishness by spending the fall and winter away from White Divide - or the sight of it - I commenced right away to find out my mistake. No sooner did the big ridge rise up from the green horizon, than every scar, and wrinkle, and abrupt little peak fairly shouted things about Beryl King.

She wasn't there; she was back in New York, and that blasted Terence Weaver was back there, too, making all kinds of love to her according to the letters of Edith. But I hadn't realized just how seriously I was taking it, till I got within sight of the ridge that had sheltered her abiding-place and had made all the trouble.

Like a fool I had kept telling myself that I was fair sick for the range; for range-horses and range-living; for the wind that always blows over the prairies, and for the cattle that feed on the hills and troop down the long coulee bottoms to drink at their favorite watering-places. I thought it was the boys I wanted to see, and to gallop out with them in the soft sunrise, and lie down with them under a tent roof at night; that I wanted to eat my meals sitting cross-legged in the grass, with my plate piled with all the courses at once and my cup of coffee balanced precariously somewhere within reach.

That's what I thought. When things tasted flat in old Frisco, I

B. M. BOWER

wasn't dead sure why, and maybe I didn't want to be sure why. When I couldn't get hold of anything that had the old tang, I laid it all to a hankering after round-up.

Even when we drove around the end of White Divide, and got up on a ridge where I could see the long arm that stretched out from the east side of King's Highway, I wouldn't own up to myself that there was the cause of all my bad feelings. I think Frosty knew, all along; for when I had sat with my face turned to the divide, and had let my cigarette go cold while I thought and thought, and remembered, he didn't say a word. But when memory came down to that last ride through the pass, and to Shylock shot down by the corral, at last to Frosty standing, tall and dark, against the first yellow streak of sunrise, while I rode on and left him afoot beside a half-dead horse, I turned my eyes and looked at his thin, thoughtful face beside me.

His eyes met mine for half a minute, and he had a little twitching at the corners of his mouth. "Chirk up," he said quietly. "The chances are she'll come back this summer."

I guess I blushed. Anyway, I didn't think of anything to say that would be either witty or squelching, and could only relight my cigarette and look the fool I felt. He'd caught me right in the solar plexus, and we both knew it, and there was nothing to say. So after awhile we commenced talking about a new bunch of horses that dad had bought through an agent, and that had to be saddle-broke that summer, and I kept my eyes away from White Divide and my mind from all it meant to me.

The old ranch did look good to me, and Perry Potter actually shook hands; if you knew him as well as I do you'd realize better what such a demonstration means, coming from a fellow like him. Why, even his lips are always shut with a drawstring - from the looks - to keep any words but what are actually necessary from coming out. His eyes have the same look, kind of pulled in at the corners. No, don't ever accuse Perry Potter of being a demonstrative man, or a loquacious one.

I had two days at the ranch, getting fitted into the life again; on the third the round-up started, and I packed a "war-bag" of essentials, took my last summer's chaps down off the nail in the bunk-house where they had hung all that time as a sort of absent-but-not-forgotten memento, one of the boys told me, and started out in full regalia and with an enthusiasm that was real - while it lasted.

If you never slept on the new grass with only a bit of canvas between you and the stars; if you have never rolled out, at daylight, and dressed before your eyes were fair open, and rushed with the bunch over to the mess-wagon for your breakfast; if you have never saddled hurriedly a range-bred and range-broken cayuse with a hump in his back and seven devils in his eye, and gone careening across the dew-wet prairie like a tug-boat in a choppy sea; if you have never - well, if you don't know what it's all like, and how it gets into the very bones of you so that the hankering never quite leaves you when you try to give it up, I'm not going to tell you. I can't. If I could, you'd know just how heady it made me feel those first few days after we started out to "work the range."

I was fond of telling myself, those days, that I'd been more scared than hurt, and that it was the range I was in love with, and not Beryl King at all. She was simply a part of it - but she wasn't the whole thing, nor even a part that was going to be indispensable to my mental comfort. I was a free man once more, and so long as I had a good horse under me, and a bunch of the right sort of fellows to lie down in the same tent with, I wasn't going to worry much over any girl.

That, for as long as a week; and that, more than pages of description, shows you how great is the spell of the range-land, and how it grips a man.

B. M. BOWER

CHAPTER XIII.

WE MEET ONCE MORE.

I think it was about three weeks that I stayed with the round-up. I didn't get tired of the life, or weary of honest labor, or anything of that sort. I think the trouble was that I grew accustomed to the life, so that the exhilarating effects of it wore off, or got so soaked into my system that I began to take it all as a matter of course. And that, naturally, left room for other things.

I know I'm no good at analysis, and that's as close as I can come to accounting for my welching, the third week out. You see, we were working south and west, and getting farther and farther away from - well, from the part of country that I knew and liked best. It's kind of lonesome, leaving old landmarks behind you; so when White Divide dropped down behind another range of hills and I couldn't turn in my saddle almost any time and see the jagged, blue sky-line of her, I stood it for about two days. Then I rolled my bed one morning, caught out two horses from my string instead of one, told the wagon-boss I was going back to the ranch, and lit out - with the whole bunch grinning after me. As they would have said, they were all "dead next," but were good enough not to say so. Or, perhaps, they remembered the boxing-lessons I had given them in the bunk-house a year or more ago.

I did feel kind of sneaking, quitting them like that; but it's like playing higher than your logical limit: you know you're doing a fool thing, and you want to plant your foot violently upon your own person somewhere, but you go right ahead in the face of it all. They didn't have to tell me I was acting like a calf that has lost his mother in the herd. (You know he is prone to go mooning back to the last place he was with her, if it's ten miles.) I knew it, all right. And when I topped a hill and saw the high ridges and peaks of White Divide stand up against the horizon to the north, I was so glad I felt ashamed of myself and called one Ellis Carleton worse names than I'd stand to hear from anybody else.

Still, to go back to the metaphor, I kept on shoving in chips, just as if I had a chance to win out and wasn't the biggest, softest-headed idiot the Lord ever made. Why, even Perry Potter almost grinned when I came riding up to the corral; and I caught the fellow that was kept on at the ranch, lowering his left lid knowingly at the cook, when I went in to supper that first night. But I was too far gone then to care much what anybody thought; so long as they kept their mouths shut and left me alone, that was all I asked of them. Oh, I was a heroic figure, all right, those days.

On a day in June I rode dispiritedly over to the little butte just out from the mouth of the pass. Not that I expected to see her; I went because I had gotten into the habit of going, and every nice morning just simply *pulled* me over that way, no matter how much I might want to keep away. That argues great strength of character for me, I know, but it's unfortunately the truth.

I knew she was back - or that she should be back, if nothing had happened to upset their plans. Edith had written me that they were all coming, and that they would have two cars, this summer, instead of just one, and that they expected to stay a month. She and her mother, and Beryl and Aunt Lodema, Terence Weaver - deuce take him! - and two other fellows, and a Gertrude - somebody - I forget just who. Edith hoped that I would make my peace with Uncle Homer, so they could see something of me. (If I had told her how easy it was to make peace with "Uncle Homer," and how he had turned me down, she might not have been quite so sure that it was all my bull-headedness.) She complained that Gertrude was engaged to one of the fellows, and so was awfully stupid; and Beryl might as well be -

I tore up the letter just there, and the wind, which was howling that day, caught the pieces and took them over into North Dakota; so I don't know what else Edith may have had to tell me. I'd read enough to put me in a mighty nasty temper at any rate, so I suppose its purpose was accomplished. Edith is like all the rest: If she can say anything to make a man uncomfortable she'll do it, every time.

This day, I remember, I went mooning along, thinking hard things about the world in general, and my little corner of it in particular. The country was beginning to irritate me, and I knew that if something didn't break loose pretty soon I'd be off somewhere. Riding over to little buttes, and not meeting a soul on the way or seeing anything but a bare rock when you get there, grows monotonous in time, and rather gets on the nerves of a fellow.

When I came close up to the butte, however, I saw a flutter of skirts on the pinnacle, and it made a difference in my gait; I went up all out of breath, scrambling as if my life hung on a few seconds, and calling myself a different kind of fool for every step I took. I kept assuring myself, over and over, that it was only Edith, and that there was no need to get excited about it. But all the while I knew, down deep down in the thumping chest of me, that it wasn't Edith. Edith couldn't make all that disturbance in my circulatory system, not in a thousand years.

She was sitting on the same rock, and she was dressed in the same adorable riding outfit with a blue wisp of veil wound somehow on her gray felt hat, and the same blue roan was dozing, with dragging bridle-reins, a few rods down the other side of the peak. She was sketching so industriously that she never heard me coming until I stood right at her elbow.

It might have been the first time over again, except that my mental attitude toward her had changed a lot.

"That's better; I can see now what you're trying to draw," I said, looking down over her shoulder - not at the sketch; it might have been a sea view, for all I knew - but at the pink curve of her cheek, which was growing pinker while I looked.

She did not glance up, or even start; so she must have known, all along, that I was headed her way. She went on making a lot of marks that didn't seem to fit anywhere, and that seemed to me a bit wobbly and uncertain. I caught just the least hint of a smile twitching the corner of her mouth - I wanted awfully to kiss it!

"Yes? I believe I have at last got everything - King's Highway - in the proper perspective and the proper proportion," she said, stumbling a bit over the alliteration - and no wonder. It was a sentence to stampede cattle; but I didn't stampede. I wanted, more than ever, to kiss - but I won't be like Barney, if I can help it.

"It's too far off - too unattainable," I criticized - meaning something more than her sketch of the pass. "And it's too narrow. If a fellow rode in there he would have to go straight on through; there wouldn't be a chance to turn back."

"Ergo, a fellow shouldn't ride in," she retorted, with a composure positively wicked, considering my feelings. "Though it does seem that a fellow rather enjoys going straight on through, regardless of anything; promises, for instance."

That was the gauntlet I'd been hoping for. From the minute I first saw her there it flashed upon me that she was astonished and indignant that night when she saw Frosty and me come charging through the pass, after me telling her I wouldn't do it any more. It looked to me like I'd have to square myself, so I

B. M. BOWER

was glad enough of the chance.

"Sometimes a fellow has to do things regardless of - promises,"
I explained. "Sometimes it's a matter of life and death. If a
fellow's father, for instance -"

"Oh, I know; Edith told me all about it." Her tone was
curious, and while it did not encourage further explanations or
apologies, it also lacked absolution of the offense I had
committed.

I sat down in the grass, half-facing her to better my chance of a
look into her eyes. I was consumed by a desire to know if they
still had the power to send crimply waves all over me. For the
rest, she was prettier even than I remembered her to be, and I
could fairly see what little sense or composure I had left slide
away from me. I looked at her fatuously, and she looked
speculatively at a sharp ridge of the divide as if that sketch were
the only thing around there that could possibly interest her.

"Why do you spend every summer out here in the wilderness?"
I asked, feeling certain that nothing but speech could save me
from going hopelessly silly.

She turned her eyes calmly toward me, and - their power had
not weakened, at all events. I felt as if I had taken hold of a
battery with all the current turned on.

"Why, I suppose I like it here in summer. You're here,
yourself; don't you like it?"

I wanted to say something smart, there, and I have thought of
a dozen bright remarks since; but at the time I couldn't think
of a blessed thing that came within a mile of being either witty
or epigrammatic. Love-making was all new to me, and I saw
right then that I wasn't going to shine. I finally did remark
that I should like it better if her father would be less belligerent
and more peaceful as a neighbor.

"You told me, last summer, that you enjoyed keeping up the feud," she reminded, smiling whimsically down at me.

She made a wrong play there; she let me see that she did remember some things that I said. It boosted my courage a notch.

"But that was last summer," I countered. "One can change one's view-point a lot in twelve months. Anyway, you knew all along that I didn't mean a word of it."

"Indeed!" It was evident that she didn't quite like having me take that tone.

"Yes, 'indeed'!" I repeated, feeling a rebellion against circumstances and at convention growing stronger within me. Why couldn't I put her on my horse and carry her off and keep her always? I wondered crazily. That was what I wanted to do.

"Do you ever mean what you say, I wonder?" she mused, biting her pencil-point like a schoolgirl when she can't remember how many times three goes into twenty-seven.

"Sometimes. Sometimes I mean more." I set my teeth, closed my eyes - mentally - and plunged, insanely, not knowing whether I should come to the surface alive or knock my head on a rock and stay down. "For instance, when I say that some day I shall carry you off and find a preacher to marry us, and that we shall live happily ever after, whether you want to or not, because I shall *make* you, I mean every word of it - and a lot more."

That was going some, I fancy! I was so scared at myself I didn't dare breathe. I kept my eyes fixed desperately on the mouth of the pass, all golden-green in the sunshine; and I remember that my teeth were so tight together that they ached afterward.

The point of her pencil came off with a snap. I heard it, but I was afraid to look. "Do you? How very odd!" Her voice

B. M. BOWER

sounded queer, as if it had been squeezed dry of every sort of emotion. "And - Edith?"

I looked at her then, fast enough. "Edith?" I stared at her stupidly. "What the - what's Edith got to do with it?"

"Possibly nothing" - in the same squeezed tone. "Men are so - er - irresponsible; and you say you don't always mean - Still, when a man writes pages and *pages* to a girl every week for nearly a year, one naturally supposes -"

"Oh, look here!" I was getting desperate enough to be a bit rough with her. "Edith doesn't care a rap about me, and you know it. And she knows I don't care, and - and if anybody had anything to say, it would be your Mr. Terence Weaver."

"*My* Mr. Terence Weaver?" She was looking down at me sidewise, in a perfectly maddening way. "You are really very - er - funny, Mr. Carleton."

"Well," I rapped out between my teeth, "I don't *feel* funny. I feel -"

"No? But, really, you know, you act that way."

I saw she was getting all the best of it - and, in my opinion, that would kill what little chance a man might have with a girl. I set deliberately about breaking through that crust of composure, if I did nothing more.

"That depends on the view-point," I grinned. "Would you think it funny if I carried you off - really, you know - and - er - married you and made you live happy -"

"You seem to insist upon the happy part of it, which is not at all -"

"Necessary?" I hinted.

"Plausible," she supplied sweetly.

"But would you think it funny, if I did?"

She regarded her broken pencil ruefully - or pretended to - and pinched her brows together in deep meditation. Oh, she was the most maddening bit of young womanhood - But, there, no Barney for me.

"I - might," she decided at last. "It *would* be rather droll, you know, and I wonder how you'd manage it; I'm not very tiny, and I rather think it wouldn't be easy to - er - carry me off. Would you wear a mask - a black velvet mask? I should insist upon black velvet. And would you say: 'Gadzooks, madam! I command you not to scream!' Would you?" She leaned toward me, and her eyes - well, for downright torture, women are at times perfectly fiendish.

I caught her hand, and I held it, too, in spite of her. That far I was master.

"No," I told her grimly. "If I saw that you were going to do anything so foolish as to scream, I should just kiss you, and - kiss you till you were glad to be sensible about it."

Well, she tried first to look calmly amused; then she tried to look insulted, and to freeze me into sanity. She ended, however, by looking a good bit confused, and by blushing scarlet. I had won that far. I kept her hand held tight in mine; I could feel it squirm to get away, and it felt - oh, thunder!

"Let's play something else," she said, after a long minute. "I - I never did admire highwaymen particularly, and I must go home."

"No, you mustn't," I contradicted. "You must -"

She looked at me with those wonderful, heavy-lashed eyes, and her lips had a little quiver as if - Oh, I don't know, but I let go her hand, and I felt like a great, hulking brute that had been teasing a child till it cried.

"All right," I sighed, "I'll let you go this time. But I warn you, little girl. If - no, *when* I find you out from King's Highway by yourself again, that kidnaping is sure going to come off. The Lord intended you to be Mrs. Ellis Carleton. And forty feuds and forty fathers can't prevent it. I don't believe in going against the decrees of Providence; a *wise* Providence."

She bit her lip at the corner. "You must have a little private Providence of your own," she retorted, with something like her old assurance. "I'm sure mine never hinted at such a - a fate for me. And one feud is as good as forty, Mr. Carleton. If you are anything like your father, I can easily understand how the feud began. The Kings and the Carletons are fond of their own way."

"Thy way shall be my way," I promised rashly, just because it sounded smart.

"Thank you. Then there will be no melodramatic abductions in the shadow of White Divide," she laughed triumphantly, "and I shall escape a most horrible fate!" She went, still laughing, down to where her horse was waiting.

I followed - rather, I kept pace with her. "All the same, I dare you to ride out alone from King's Highway again," I defied. "For, if you do, and I find you -"

"Good-by, Mr. Carleton. You'd be splendid in vaudeville," she mocked from her saddle, where she had got with all the ease of a cowboy, without any help from me. "Black velvet mask and gadzooks, madam - I must certainly tell Edith. It will amuse her, I'm sure."

"No, you won't tell Edith," I flung after her, but I don't know if she heard.

She rode away down the steep slope, the roan leaning back stiffly against the incline, and I stood watching her like a fool. I didn't think it would be good policy to follow her. I tried to roll a cigarette - in case she might look back to see how I was taking her last shot. But she didn't, and I threw the thing away half-made. It was a case where smoke wouldn't help me.

If I hadn't made my chance any better, I knew I couldn't very well make it worse; but there was mighty little comfort in that reflection. And what a bluff I had put up! Carry her off and marry her? Lord knows I wanted to, badly enough! But -

CHAPTER XIV.

FROSTY DISAPPEARS.

On the way back to the ranch I overtook Frosty mooning along at a walk, with his shoulders humped in the way a man has when he's thinking pretty hard. I had left Frosty with the round-up, and I was pretty much surprised to see him here. I didn't feel in the mood for conversation, even with him; but, to be decent, I spurred up alongside and said hello, and where had he come from? There was nothing in that for a man to get uppish about, but he turned and actually glared at me.

"I might be an inquisitive son-of-a-gun and ask you the same thing," he growled.

"Yes, you might," I agreed. "But, if you did, I'd be apt to tell you to depart immediately for a place called Gehenna - which is polite for hell."

"Well, same here," he retorted laconically; and that ended our conversation, though we rode stirrup to stirrup for eight miles.

I can't say that, after the first shock of surprise, I gave much time to wondering what brought Frosty home. I took it he had had a row with the wagon-boss. Frosty is an independent sort and won't stand a word from anybody, and the wagon-boss is something of a bully. The gait they were traveling, out there with the wagons, was fraying the nerves of the whole bunch before I left. And that was all I thought about Frosty.

I had troubles of my own, about that time. I had put up my bluff, and I kept wondering what I should do if Beryl King called me. There wasn't much chance that she would, of course; but, still, she wasn't that kind of girl who always does the conventional thing and the expected thing, and I had seen a gleam in her eyes that, in a man's, I should call deviltry, pure and simple. If I should meet her out somewhere, and she even *looked* a dare - I'll confess one thing: for a whole week I was mighty shy of riding out where I would be apt to meet her; and you can call me a coward if you like.

Still, I had schemes, plenty of them. I wanted her - Lord knows how I wanted her! - and I got pretty desperate, sometimes. Once I saddled up with the fixed determination of riding boldly - and melodramatically - into King's Highway, facing old King, and saying: "Sir, I love your daughter. Let bygones be bygones. Dad and I forgive you, and hope you will do the same. Let us have peace, and let me have Beryl -" or something to that effect.

He'd only have done one of two things; he'd have taken a shot at me, or he'd have told me to go to the same old place where we consign unpleasant people. But I didn't tempt him, though I did tempt fate. I went over to the little butte, climbed it pensively, and sat on the flat rock and gazed forlornly at the mouth of the pass.

I had the rock to myself, but I made a discovery that set the nerves of me jumping like a man just getting over a - well, a season of dissipation. In the sandy soil next the rock were many confused footprints - the prints of little riding-boots; and they looked quite fresh. She had been there, all right, and I had missed her! I swore, and wondered what she must think of me. Then I had an inspiration. I rolled and half-smoked eight cigarettes, and scattered the stubs with careful carelessness in the immediate vicinity of the rock. I put my boots down in a clear spot of sand where they left marks that fairly shouted of my presence. Then I walked off a few steps and studied the effect with much satisfaction. When she came again, she couldn't fail to see that I had been there; that I had waited a long time - she could count the cigarette stubs and so form some estimate of the time - and had gone away, presumably in deep disappointment. Maybe it would make her feel a little less sure of herself, to know that I was camping thus earnestly on her trail. I rode home, feeling a good deal better in my mind.

That night it rained barrelsful. I laid and listened to it, and gritted my teeth. Where was all my cunning now? Where were those blatant footprints of mine that were to give their own eloquent message? I could imagine just how the water was running in yellow streams off the peak of that butte. Then it came to me that, at all events, some of the cigarette-stubs would be left; so I turned over and went to sleep.

I wish to say, before I forget it, that I don't think I am deceitful by nature. You see, it changes a fellow a lot to get all tangled up in his feelings over a girl that doesn't seem to care a rap for you. He does things that are positively idiotic At any rate, I did. And I could sympathize some with Barney MacTague; only, his girl had a crooked nose and no eyebrows to speak of, so he hadn't the excuse that I had. Take a girl with eyes like Beryl -

A couple of days after that - days when I hadn't the nerve to go near the little butte - Frosty drew six months' wages and disappeared without a word to anybody. He didn't come back that night, and the next day Perry Potter, who knows well the strange freaks cowboys will sometimes take when they have been working steadily for a long time, suggested that I ride over to Kenmore and see if Frosty was there, and try my powers of persuasion on him - unless he was already broke; in which case, according to Perry Potter, he would come back without any persuading. Perry Potter added dryly that it wouldn't be out of my way any, and would only be a little longer ride. I must say I looked at him with suspicion. The way that little dried-up sinner found out everything was positively uncanny.

Frosty, as I soon discovered, was not in Kenmore. He had been, for I learned by inquiring around that he had passed the night there at that one little hotel. Also that he had, not more than two hours before - or three, at most - hired a rig and driven on to Osage. A man told me that he had taken a lady with him; but, knowing Frosty as I did, I couldn't quite swallow that. It was queer, though, about his hiring a rig and leaving his saddle-horse there in the stable. I couldn't understand it, but I wasn't going to buy into Frosty's affairs unless I had to. I ate my dinner dejectedly in the hotel - the dinner was enough to make any man dejected - and started home again.

B. M. BOWER

CHAPTER XV.

THE BROKEN MOTOR-CAR.

Out where the trail from Kenmore intersects the one leading from Laurel to and through King's Highway, I passed over a little hill and came suddenly upon a big, dark-gray touring-car stalled in the road. In it Beryl King sat looking intently down at her toes. I nearly fell off my horse at the shock of it, and then my blood got to acting funny, so that my head felt queer. Then I came to, and rode boldly up to her, mentally shaking hands with myself over my good luck. For it was good luck just to see her, whether anything came of it or not.

"Something wrong with the wheelbarrow?" I asked her, with a placid superiority.

She looked up with a little start - she never did seem to feel my presence until I spoke to her - and frowned prettily; but whether at me or at the car, I didn't know.

"I guess something must be," she answered quite meekly, for her. "It keeps making the funniest buzz when I start it - and it's Mr. Weaver's car, and he doesn't know - I - I borrowed it without asking, and -"

"That car is all right," I bluffed from my saddle. "It's simply obeying instructions. It comes under the jurisdiction of my private Providence, you see. I ordered it that you should be here, and in distress, and grateful for my helping hand." How was that for straight nerve?

"Well, then, let's have the helping hand and be done. I should be at home, by now. They will wonder - I just went for a - a little spin, and when I turned to go back, it started that funny noise. I - I'm afraid of it. It - might blow up, or - or something."

She seemed in a strangely explanatory mood, that was, to say the least, suspicious. Either she had come out purposely to torment me, or she was afraid of what she knew was in my mind, and wanted to make me forget it. But my mettle was up for good. I had no notion of forgetting, or of letting her.

"I'll do what I can, and willingly," I told her coolly. "It looks like a good car - an accommodating car. I hope you are prepared to pay the penalty -"

"Penalty?" she interrupted, and opened her eyes at me innocently; a bit *too* innocently, I may say.

"Penalty; yes. The penalty of letting me find you outside of King's Highway, *alone*," I explained brazenly.

She tried a lever hurriedly, and the car growled up at her so that she quit. Then she pulled herself together and faced me nonchalantly.

"Oh-h. You mean about the black velvet mask? I'm afraid - I had forgotten that funny little - joke." With all she could do, her face and her tone were not convincing.

I gathered courage as she lost it. "I see that I must demonstrate to you the fact that I am not altogether a joke," I said grimly, and got down from my horse.

I don't, to this day, know what she imagined I was going to do. She sat very still; the kind of stillness a rabbit adopts when he hopes to escape the notice of an enemy. I could see that she

B. M. BOWER

hardly breathed, even.

But when I reached her, I only got a wrench out of the tool-box and yanked open the hood to see what ailed the motor. I knew something of that make of car; in fact, I had owned one before I got the *Yellow Peril*, and I had a suspicion that there wasn't much wrong; a loosened nut will sometimes sound a good deal more serious than it really is. Still, a half-formed idea - a perfectly crazy idea - made me go over the whole machine very carefully to make sure she was all right.

When I was through I stood up and found that she was regarding me curiously, yet with some amusement. She seemed to feel herself mistress of the situation, and to consider me as an interesting plaything. I didn't approve that attitude.

"At all events," she said when she met my eyes, and speaking as if there had been no break in our conversation, "you are rather a *good* joke. Thank you so much."

I put away the wrench, fastened the lid of the tool-box, and then I faced her grimly. "I see mere words are wasted on you," I said. "I shall have to carry you off - Beryl King; I *shall* carry you off if you look at me that way again!"

She did look that way, only more so. I wonder what she thought a man was made of, to stand it. I set my teeth hard together.

"Have you got the - er - the black velvet mask?" she taunted, leaning just the least bit toward me. Her eyes - I say it deliberately - were a direct challenge that no man could refuse to accept and feel himself a man after.

"Mask or no mask - you'll see!" I turned away to where my horse was standing eying the car with extreme disfavor, picked up the reins, and glanced over my shoulder; I didn't know but she would give me the slip. She was sitting very straight, with both hands on the wheel and her eyes looking straight before her. She might have been posing for a photograph, from the look of her. I tied the reins with a quick twist over the saddle-horn and gave him a slap on the rump. I knew he would go straight home. Then I went back and stepped into the car just as she reached down and started the motor. If she had meant to run away from me she had been just a second too late. She gave me a sidelong, measuring glance, and gasped. The car slid easily along the trail as if it were listening for what we were going to say.

"I shall drive," I announced quietly, taking her hands gently from the wheel. She moved over to make room mechanically, as if she didn't in the least understand this new move of mine. I know she never dreamed of what was really in my heart to do.

"You will drive - where?" her voice was politely freezing.

"To find that preacher, of course," I answered, trying to sound surprised that she should ask, I sent the speed up a notch.

"You - you never would *dare*!" she cried breathlessly, and a little anxiously.

"The deuce I wouldn't!" I retorted, and laughed in the face of her. It was queer, but my thoughts went back, for just a flash, to the time Barney had dared me to drive the *Yellow Peril* up past the Cliff House to Sutro Baths. I had the same heady elation of daredeviltry. I wouldn't have turned back, then, even if I hadn't cared so much for her.

She didn't say anything more, and I sent the car ahead at a pace that almost matched the mood I was in, and that brought White Divide sprinting up to meet us. The trail was good, and the car was a dandy. I was making straight for King's Highway as the best and only chance of carrying out my foolhardy design. I doubt if any bold, bad knight of old ever had the effrontery to carry his lady-love straight past her own door in broad daylight.

Yet it was the safest thing I could do. I meant to get to Osage, and the only practicable route for a car lay through the pass. To be sure, there was a preacher at Kenmore; but with the chance of old King being there also and interrupting the ceremony - supposing I brought matters successfully that far - with a shot or two, did not in the least appeal to me. I had made sure that there was plenty of gasoline aboard, so I drove her right along.

"I hope your father isn't home," I remarked truthfully when we were slipping into the wide jaws of the pass.

"He is, though; and so is Mr. Weaver. I think you had better jump out here and run home, or it is not a velvet mask you will need, but a mantle of invisibility." I couldn't make much of her tone, but her words implied that even yet she would not take me seriously.

"Well, I've neither mask nor mantle," I said, "But the way I can fade down the pass will, I think, be a fair substitute for both."

She said nothing whatever to that, but she began to seem interested in the affair - as she had need to be. She might have jumped out and escaped while I was down opening the gate - but she didn't. She sat quite still, as if we were only out on a commonplace little jaunt. I wondered if she didn't have the spirit of adventure in her make-up, also. Girls do, sometimes. When I had got in again, I turned to her, remembering something.

"Gadzooks, madam! I command you not to scream," I quoted sternly.

At that, for the first time in our acquaintance, she laughed; such a delicious, rollicky little laugh that I felt ready, at the sound, to face a dozen fathers and they all old Kings.

As we came chugging up to the house, several faces appeared in the doorway as if to welcome and scold the runaway. I saw old King with his pipe in his mouth; and there were Aunt Lodema and Weaver. They were all smiling at the escapade - Beryl's escapade, that is - and I don't think they realized just at first who I was, or that I was in any sense a menace to their peace of mind.

When we came opposite and showed no disposition to stop, or even to slow up, I saw the smiles freeze to amazement, and then - but I hadn't the time to look. Old King yelled something, but by that time we were skidding around the first shed, where Shylock had been shot down on my last trip through there. It was a new shed, I observed mechanically as we went by. I heard much shouting as we disappeared, but by that time we were almost through the gantlet. I made the last turn on two wheels, and scudded away up the open trail of the pass.

B. M. BOWER

CHAPTER XVI.

ONE MORE RACE.

A faint toot-toot warned from behind.

"They've got out the other car," said Beryl, a bit tremulously; and added, "it's a much bigger one than this."

I let her out all I dared for the road we were traveling; and then there we were, at that blessed gate. I hadn't thought of it till we were almost upon it, but it didn't take much thought; there was only one thing to do, and I did it.

I caught Beryl by an arm and pulled her down to the floor of the car, not taking my eyes from the trail, or speaking. Then I drove the car forward like a cannon-ball. We hit that gate like a locomotive, and scarcely felt the jar. I knew the make of that motor, and what it could do. The air was raining splinters and bits of lamps, but we went right on as if nothing had happened, and as fast as the winding trail would allow. I knew that beyond the pass the road ran straight and level for many a mile, and that we could make good time if we got the chance.

Beryl sat half-turned in the seat, glancing back; but for me, I was busy watching the trail and taking the sharp turns in a way to lift the hair of one not used to traveling by lightning. I will confess it was ticklish going, at that pace, and there were places when I took longer chances than I had any right to take. But, you see, I had Beryl - and I meant to keep her.

That Weaver fellow must have had a bigger bump of caution than I, or else he'd never raced. I could hear them coming, but they didn't seem to be gaining; rather, they lost ground, if anything. Presently Beryl spoke again, still looking back.

"Don't you think, Mr. Carleton, this joke has gone far enough? You have demonstrated what you *could* do, if -"

I risked both our lives to glance at her. "This joke," I said, "is going to Osage. I want to marry you, and you know it. The Lord and this car willing, I'm going to. Still, if you really have been deceived in my intentions, and insist upon going back, I shall stop, of course, and give you back to your father. But you must do it now, at once, or - marry me."

She gave me a queer, side glance, but she did not insist. Naturally I didn't stop, either.

We shot out into the open, with the windings of the pass behind, and then I turned the old car loose, and maybe we didn't go! She wasn't a bad sort - but I would have given a good deal, just then, if she had been the *Yellow Peril* stripped for a race. I could hear the others coming up, and we were doing all we could; I saw to that.

"I think they'll catch us," Beryl observed maliciously. "Their car is a sixty h.p. Mercedes, and this -"

"Is about a forty," I cut in tartly, not liking the tone of her; "and just plain American make. But don't you fret, my money's on Uncle Sam."

She said no more; indeed, it wasn't easy to talk, with the wind drawing the breath right out of your lungs. She hung onto her hat, and to the seat, and she had her hands full, let me tell you.

The purr of their motor grew louder, and I didn't like the sound of it a bit. I turned my head enough to see them slithering along close - abominably close. I glimpsed old King in the tonneau, and Weaver humped over the wheel in an unpleasantly businesslike fashion.

I humped over my own wheel and tried to coax her up a bit, as if she had been the *Yellow Peril* at the wind-up of a close race. For a minute I felt hopeful. Then I could tell by the sound that Weaver was crowding up.

"They're gaining, Mr. Carleton!" Beryl's voice had a new ring in it, and I caught my breath.

"Can you get here and take the wheel and hold her straight without slowing her?" I asked, looking straight ahead. The trail was level and not a bend in it for half a mile or so, and I thought there was a chance for us. "I've a notion that friend Weaver has nerves. I'm going to rattle him, if I can; but whatever happens, don't loose your grip and spill us out. I won't hurt them."

Her hands came over and touched mine on the wheel. "I've raced a bit myself," she said simply. "I can drive her straight."

I wriggled out of the way and stood up, glancing down to make sure she was all right. She certainly didn't look much like the girl who was afraid because something "made a funny noise." I suspected that she knew a lot about motors.

A bullet clipped close. Beryl set her teeth into her lips, but grittily refrained from turning to look. I breathed freer.

"Now, don't get scared," I warned, balanced myself as well as I could in the swaying car, and sent a shot back at them.

Weaver came up to my expectations. He ducked, and the car swerved out of the trail and went wavering spitefully across the prairie. Old King sent another rifle-bullet my way - I must have made a fine mark, standing up there - and he was a good shot. I was mighty glad he was getting jolted enough to spoil his aim.

Weaver came to himself a bit and grabbed frantically for brake and throttle and steering-wheel all at once, it looked like. He was rattled, all right; he must have given the wheel a twist the wrong way, for their car hit a jutting rock and went up in the air like a pitching bronco, and old King sailed in a beautiful curve out of the tonneau.

I was glad Beryl didn't see that. I watched, not breathing, till I saw Weaver scramble into view, and Beryl's dad get slowly to his feet and grope about for his rifle; so I knew there would be no funeral come of it. I fancy his language was anything but mild, though by that time we were too far away to hear anything but the faint churning of their motor as their wheels pawed futilely in the air.

They were harmless for the present. Their car tilted ungracefully on its side, and, though I hadn't any quarrel with Weaver, I hoped his big Mercedes was out of business. I put away my gun, sat down, and looked at Beryl.

She was very white around the mouth, and her hat was hanging by one pin, I remember; but her eyes were fixed unswervingly upon the brown trail stretching lazily across the green of the grass-land, and she was driving that big car like an old hand.

"Well?" her voice was clear, and anxious, and impatient.

"It's all right," I said. I took the wheel from her, got into her place, and brought the car down to a six-mile gait. "It's all right," I repeated triumphantly. "They're out of the race - for awhile, at least, and not hurt, that I could see. Just plain, old-fashioned mad. Don't look like that, Beryl!" I slowed the car more. "You're glad, aren't you? And you *will* marry me, dear?"

She leaned back panting a little from the strain of the last half-hour, and did things to her hat. I watched her furtively. Then she let her eyes meet mine; those dear, wonderful eyes of hers! And her mouth was half-smiling, and very tender.

B. M. BOWER

"You *silly*!" That's every word she said, on my oath.

But I stopped that car dead still and gathered her into my arms, and - Oh, well, I won't trail off into sentiment, you couldn't appreciate it if I did.

It's a mercy Weaver's car *was* done for, or they could have walked right up and got their hands on us before we'd have known it.

CHAPTER XVII.

THE FINAL RECKONING.

About four o'clock we reached the ferry, just behind a fagged-out team and a light buggy that had in it two figures - one of whom, at least, looked familiar to me.

"Frosty, by all that's holy!" I exclaimed when we came close enough to recognize a man. "I clean forgot, but I was sent to Kenmore this morning to find that very fellow."

"Don't you know the other?" Beryl laughed teasingly. "I was at their wedding this morning, and wished them God-speed. I never dreamed I should be God-speeded myself, directly! I drove Edith, over to Kenmore quite early in the car, and -"

"Edith!"

"Certainly, Edith. Whom else? Did you think she would be left behind, pining at your infidelity? Didn't you know they are old, old sweethearts who had quarreled and parted quite like a story? She used to read your letters so eagerly to see if you made any remark about him; you did, quite often, you know. I drove her over to Kenmore, and afterward went off toward Laurel just to put in the time and not arrive home too soon without her - which might have been awkward, if father took a notion to go after her. I'm so glad we came up with them." She stood up and waved her hand at Edith.

B. M. BOWER

I shouted reassurances to Frosty, who was looking apprehensively back at us. But it was a facer. I had never once suspected them of such a thing.

"Well," I greeted, when we overtook them and could talk comfortably; "this is luck. When we get across to Pochette's you can get in with us, Mr. and Mrs. Miller, and add the desired touch of propriety to *our* wedding."

They did some staring themselves, then, and Beryl blushed delightfully - just as she did everything else. She was growing an altogether bewitching bit of femininity, and I kept thanking my private Providence that I had had the nerve to kidnap her first and take chances on her being willing. Honest, I don't believe I'd ever have got her in any other way.

When we stopped at Pochette's door the girls ran up and tangled their arms around each other and wasted enough kisses to make Frosty and me swear. And they whispered things, and then laughed about it, and whispered some more, and all we could hear was a gurgle of "You dear!" and the like of that. Frosty and I didn't do much; we just looked at each other and grinned. And it's long odds we understood each other quite as well as the girls did after they'd whispered and gurgled an hour.

We had an early dinner - or supper - and ate fried bacon and stewed prunes - and right there I couldn't keep the joke, but had to tell the girls about how Frosty and I had deviled Beryl's father, that time. They could see the point, all right, and they seemed to appreciate it, too.

After that, we all talked at once, sometimes; and sometimes we wouldn't have a thing to say - times when the girls would look at each other and smile, with their eyes all shiny. Frosty and I would look at them, and then at each other; and Frosty's eyes were shiny, too.

Then we went on, with the motor purring love-songs and

sliding the miles behind us, while Frosty and Edith cooed in the tonneau behind us, and didn't thank us to look around or interrupt. Beryl and I didn't say much; I was driving as fast as was wise, and sometimes faster. There was always the chance that the other car would come slithering along on our trail. Besides, it was enough just to know that this was real, and that Beryl would marry me just as soon as we found a preacher. There was no incentive to linger along the road.

It yet lacked an hour of sunset when we slid into Osage and stopped before a little goods-box church, with a sample of the same style of architecture chucked close against one side.

We left the girls with the preacher's wife, and Frosty wrote down our ages - Beryl was twenty-one, if you're curious - and our parents' names and where we were born, and if we were black or white, and a few other impertinent things which he, having been through it himself, insisted was necessary. Then he hustled out after the license, while I went over to the dry-goods and jewelry store to get a ring. I will say that Osage puts up a mighty poor showing of wedding-rings.

We were married. I suppose I ought to stop now and describe just how it was, and what the bride wore, and a list of the presents. But it didn't last long enough to be clear in my mind. Everything is a bit hazy, just there. I dropped the ring, I know that for certain, because it rolled under an article of furniture that looked suspiciously like a folding-bed masquerading as a cabinet, and Frosty had to get down on all fours and fish it out before we could go on. And Edith put her handkerchief to her mouth and giggled disreputably. But, anyway, we got married.

The preacher gave Beryl an impressive lily-and-rose certificate, which caused her much embarrassment, because it would not go into any pocket of hers or mine, but must be carried ostentatiously in the hand. I believe Edith was a bit jealous of that beflowered roll. *Her* preacher had been out of certificates, and had made shift with a plain, undecorated sheet of foolscap that Frosty said looked exactly like a home-made bill of sale. I

B. M. BOWER

told Edith she could paint some lilies around the edge, and she flounced out with her nose in the air.

We had decided that we must go back in the morning and face the music. We had no desire to be arrested for stealing Weaver's car, and there was not a man in Osage who could be trusted to drive it back. Then the girls needed a lot of things; and though Frosty had intended to take the next train East, I persuaded him to go back and wait for us.

Beryl said she was almost sure her father would be nice about it, now there was no good in being anything else. I think that long roll of stiff paper went a long way toward strengthening her confidence; she simply could not conceive of any father being able to resist its appeal and its look of finality.

We all got into the car again, and went up to the station, so I might send a wire to dad. It seemed only right and fair to let him know at once that he had a daughter to be proud of.

"Good Lord!" I broke out, when we were nearly to the depot "If that isn't - do any of you notice anything out on the side-track, over there?" I pointed an unsteady finger toward the purple and crimson sunset.

"A maroon-colored car, with dark-green -" Beryl began promptly.

"That's it," I cut in. "I was afraid joy had gone to my head and was making me see crooked. It's dad's car, the *Shasta*. And I wonder how the deuce she got *here*!"

"Probably by the railroad," said Edith flippantly.

I drove over to the *Shasta*, and we stopped. I couldn't for the life of me understand her being, there. I stared up at the windows, and nodded dazedly to Crom, grinning down at me. The next minute, dad himself came out on the platform.

"So it's you, Ellie?" he greeted calmly. "I thought Potter wasn't to let you know I was coming; he must be getting garrulous as he grows old. However, since you are here, I'm very glad to see you, my boy."

"Hello, dad," I said meekly, and helped Beryl out. I wasn't at all sure that I was glad to see him, just then. Telling dad face to face was a lot different from telling him by telegraph. I swallowed.

"Dad, let me introduce you to Miss - Mrs. Beryl King - that is, Carleton; my *wife*." I got that last word out plain enough, at any rate.

Dad stared. For once I had rather floored him. But he's a thoroughbred, all right; you can't feaze him for longer than ten seconds, and then only in extreme cases. He leaned down over the rail and held out his hand to her.

"I'm very glad to meet you, Mrs. Beryl King - that is, Carleton," he said, mimicking me. "Come up and give your dad-in-law a proper welcome."

Beryl did. I wondered how long it had been since dad had been kissed like that. It made me gulp once or twice to think of all he had missed.

Frosty and Edith came up, then, and Edith shook hands with dad and I introduced Frosty. Five minutes, there on the platform, went for explanations. Dad didn't say much; he just listened and sized up the layout. Then he led us through the vestibule into the drawing-room. And I knew, from the look of him, that we would get his verdict straight. But it was a relief not to see his finger-tips together.

"Perry Potter wrote me something of all this," he observed, settling himself comfortably in his pet chair. "He said this young cub needed looking after, or King - your father, Mrs. Carleton - would have him by the heels. I thought I'd better come and see what particular brand of - er -

"As for the motor, I might make shift to take it back myself, seeing Potter hasn't got a rig here to meet me. And if you'd like a little jaunt in the *Shasta*, you four, you're welcome to her for a couple of weeks or so. I'm not going back right away. Ellis has done his da - er - is married and off my hands, so I can take a vacation too. I can arrange transportation over any lines you want, before I start for the ranch. Will that do?"

I guess he found that it would, from the way Edith and Beryl made for him.

Frosty glanced out of the window and motioned to me. I looked, and we both bolted for the door, reaching it just as old King's foot was on the lower step of the platform. Weaver, looking like chief mourner at a funeral, was down below in his car. King came up another step, glaring and evidently in a mood for war and extermination.

"How d'y' do, King?" Dad greeted over my shoulder, before I could say a word. He may not have had his finger-tips together, but he had the finger-tip tone, all right, and I knew it was a good man who would get the better of him. "Out looking for strays? Come right up; I've got two brand new married couples here, and I need some sane person pretty bad to help me out." There was the faintest possible accent on the *sane*.

Say, it was the finest thing I had ever seen dad do. And it wasn't what he said, so much as the way he said it. I knew then why he had such, a record for getting his own way.

King swallowed hard and glared from dad to me, and then at Beryl, who had come up and laid my arm over her shoulder - where it was perfectly satisfied to stay. There was a half-minute when I didn't know whether King would shoot somebody, or have apoplexy.

"You're late, father," said Beryl sweetly, displaying that blessed certificate rather conspicuously. "If you had only hurried a little, you might have been in time for the we-wedding."

I squeezed my arm tight in approval, and came near choking her. King gasped as if somebody had an arm around his neck, too, and was squeezing.

"Oh, well, you're here now, and it's all right," put in dad easily, as though everything was quite commonplace and had happened dozens of times to us. "Crom will have dinner ready soon, though as he and Tony weren't notified that there would be a wedding-party here, I can't promise the feast I'd like to. Still, there's a bottle or two good enough to drink even *their* happiness in, Homer. Just send your chauffeur down to the town, and come in." (Good one on Weaver, that - and, the best part of it was, he heard it.)

King hesitated while I could count ten - if I I counted fast enough - and came in, following us all back through the vestibule. Inside, he looked me over and drew his hand down over his mouth; I think to hide a smile.

"Young man, yuh seem born to leave a path uh destruction behind yuh," he said. "There's a lot uh fixing to be done on that gate - and I don't reckon I ever *will* find the padlock again."

His eyes met the keen, steady look of dad, stopped there, wavered, softened to friendliness. Their hands went out half-shyly and met. "Kids are sure terrors, these days," he remarked, and they laughed a little. "Us old folks have got to stand in the corners when they're around."

*   *   *   *   *

King's Highway is open trail. Beryl and I go through there often in the *Yellow Peril*, since dad gave me outright the Bay State Ranch and all pertaining thereto - except, of course,

Perry Potter; he stays on of his own accord.

Frosty is father King's foreman, and Aunt Lodema went back East and stayed there. She writes prim little letters to Beryl, once in awhile, and I gather that she doesn't approve of the match at all. But Beryl does, and, if you ask me, I approve also. So what does anything else matter?

Choose from Thousands of 1stWorldLibrary Classics By

Adolphus WilliamWard
Aesop
Agatha Christie
Alexander Aaronsohn
Alexander Kielland
Alexandre Dumas
Alfred Gatty
Alfred Ollivant
Alice Duer Miller
Alice Turner Curtis
Alice Dunbar
Ambrose Bierce
Amelia E. Barr
Andrew Lang
Andrew McFarland Davis
Anna Sewell
Annie Besant
Annie Hamilton Donnell
Annie Payson Call
Anton Chekhov
Arnold Bennett
Arthur Conan Doyle
Arthur Ransome
Atticus
B. M. Bower
Basil King
Bayard Taylor
Ben Macomber
Booth Tarkington
Bram Stoker
C. Collodi
C. E. Orr
C. M. Ingleby
Carolyn Wells
Catherine Parr Traill
Charles A. Eastman
Charles Dickens
Charles Dudley Warner
Charles Farrar Browne
Charles Ives
Charles Kingsley
Charles Lathrop Pack
Charles Whibley
Charles Willing Beale
Charlotte M. Braeme
Charlotte M.Yonge
Clair W. Hayes
Clarence Day Jr.
Clarence E. Mulford

Clemence Housman
Confucius
Cornelis DeWitt Wilcox
Cyril Burleigh
D. H. Lawrence
Daniel Defoe
David Garnett
Don Carlos Janes
Donald Keyhole
Dorothy Kilner
Dougan Clark
E. Nesbit
E.P.Roe
E. Phillips Oppenheim
Edgar Allan Poe
Edgar Rice Burroughs
Edith Wharton
Edward J. O'Biren
John Cournos
Edwin L. Arnold
Eleanor Atkins
Elizabeth Cleghorn
Gaskell
Elizabeth Von Arnim
Ellem Key
Emily Dickinson
Erasmus W. Jones
Ernie Howard Pie
Ethel Turner
Ethel Watts Mumford
Eugenie Foa
Eugene Wood
Evelyn Everett-Green
Everard Cotes
F. J. Cross
Federick Austin Ogg
Ferdinand Ossendowski
Francis Bacon
Francis Darwin
Frances Hodgson Burnett
Frank Gee Patchin
Frank Harris
Frank Jewett Mather
Frank L. Packard
Frederick Trevor Hill
Frederick Winslow Taylor
Friedrich Kerst
Friedrich Nietzsche
Fyodor Dostoyevsky

Gabrielle E. Jackson
Garrett P. Serviss
Gaston Leroux
George Ade
Geroge Bernard Shaw
George Ebers
George Eliot
George MacDonald
George Orwell
George Tucker
George W. Cable
George Wharton James
Gertrude Atherton
Grace E. King
Grant Allen
Guillermo A. Sherwell
Gulielma Zollinger
Gustav Flaubert
H. A. Cody
H. B. Irving
H. G. Wells
H. H. Munro
H. Irving Hancock
H. Rider Haggard
H. W. C. Davis
Hamilton Wright Mabie
Hans Christian Andersen
Harold Avery
Harold McGrath
Harriet Beecher Stowe
Harry Houidini
Helent Hunt Jackson
Helen Nicolay
Hendy David Thoreau
Henrik Ibsen
Henry Adams
Henry Ford
Henry Frost
Henry James
Henry Jones Ford
Henry Seton Merriman
Henry Wadsworth
Longfellow
Henry W Longfellow
Herbert A. Giles
Herbert N. Casson
Herman Hesse
Homer
Honore De Balzac

Horace Walpole
Horatio Alger, Jr.
Howard Pyle
Howard R. Garis
Hugh Lofting
Hugh Walpole
Humphry Ward
Ian Maclaren
Israel Abrahams
J.G.Austin
J. Henri Fabre
J. M. Barrie
J. Macdonald Oxley
J. S. Knowles
J. Storer Clouston
Jack London
Jacob Abbott
James Allen
James Lane Allen
James Andrews
James Baldwin
James DeMille
James Joyce
James Oliver Curwood
James Oppenheim
James Otis
Jane Austen
Jens Peter Jacobsen
Jerome K. Jerome
John Burroughs
John F. Kennedy
John Gay
John Glasworthy
John Habberton
John Joy Bell
John Milton
John Philip Sousa
Jonathan Swift
Joseph Carey
Joseph Conrad
Joseph Jacobs
Julian Hawthrone
Julies Vernes
Justin Huntly McCarthy
Kakuzo Okakura
Kenneth Grahame
Kate Langley Bosher
L. A. Abbot
L. T. Meade
L. Frank Baum
Laura Lee Hope

Laurence Housman
Leo Tolstoy
Leonid Andreyev
Lewis Carroll
Lilian Bell
Lloyd Osbourne
Louis Tracy
Louisa May Alcott
Lucy Fitch Perkins
Lucy Maud Montgomery
Lydia Miller Middleton
Lyndon Orr
M. H. Adams
Margaret E. Sangster
Margaret Vandercook
Maria Edgeworth
Maria Thompson Daviess
Mariano Azuela
Marion Polk Angellotti
Mark Overton
Mark Twain
Mary Austin
Mary Cole
Mary Rowlandson
Mary Wollstonecraft
Shelley
Max Beerbohm
Myra Kelly
Nathaniel Hawthrone
O. F. Walton
Oscar Wilde
Owen Johnson
P.G.Wodehouse
Paul and Mable Thorn
Paul G. Tomlinson
Paul Severing
Peter B. Kyne
Plato
R. Derby Holmes
R. L. Stevenson
Rabindranath Tagore
Rahul Alvares
Ralph Waldo Emmerson
Rene Descartes
Rex E. Beach
Richard Harding Davis
Richard Jefferies
Robert Barr
Robert Frost
Robert Gordon Anderson
Robert L. Drake

Robert Lansing
Robert Michael Ballantyne
Robert W. Chambers
Rosa Nouchette Carey
Ross Kay
Rudyard Kipling
Samuel B. Allison
Samuel Hopkins Adams
Sarah Bernhardt
Selma Lagerlof
Sherwood Anderson
Sigmund Freud
Standish O'Grady
Stanley Weyman
Stella Benson
Stephen Crane
Stewart Edward White
Stijn Streuvels
Swami Abhedananda
Swami Parmananda
T. S. Ackland
The Princess Der Ling
Thomas A. Janvier
Thomas A Kempis
Thomas Anderton
Thomas Bailey Aldrich
Thomas Bulfinch
Thomas De Quincey
Thomas H. Huxley
Thomas Hardy
Thomas More
Thornton W. Burgess
U. S. Grant
Valentine Williams
Victor Appleton
Virginia Woolf
Walter Scott
Washington Irving
Wilbur Lawton
Wilkie Collins
Willa Cather
Willard F. Baker
William Makepeace
Thackeray
William W. Walter
Winston Churchill
Yei Theodora Ozaki
Young E. Allison
Zane Grey

www.ingramcontent.com/pod-product-compliance
Lightning Source LLC
Chambersburg PA
CBHW051840170626
46807CB00003B/1280